TITLE

A QUEST FOR FREEDOM

Written By: Joseph Agnes

Editing/Formatting by Get It Write Editing Co.
(www.getitwriteeditingco.com)

First Edition

JUPITA'S BIZNES in collaboration with BLACK BLYSS ENTERTAINMENT

FREETOWN,SIERRA LEONE.

Thank you, God Almighty. I am blessed with your gift of grace. I never thought I would have the wings to fly until you pushed me off a cliff edge.

To those reading this book: To every man there is a gift, and your gift will make room for you.

I can't forget you, my boss, Mrs. Elizabeth Sonney-Joe, for your advice played a vital role in this project.

Special friends worthy of remembering are Mr. and Mrs. Rev Margaret Songu. Your hearts are beautiful together and towards others. Thanks for your support.

To a very dutiful and kind-hearted mother, Mrs. Agatha Songu Benjamin: Thanks for your support.

To Mr. Abdul Karim Newland: With honesty, I must tell you I admire your works, and whenever I think of your motivations, it pushes me closer to my goal.

EVERYTHING IS POSSIBLE

I am dedicating this book to a woman I loved so much, Mrs. Miatta Swarray Gembeh. Though you have gone to that beautiful place where we all belong, the last moment I spent with you and the few sentences that you made inspire me more. "I wish I was educated. I would have written many books about life for women in Africa," you said. For you to live over a hundred years in Africa, and gave birth to more than nine children, you had a great experience and inspired many women. I loved you more than my mother {your daughter}, and I love your daughter {my mother} just as I love you. I have started writing some of the books you wished to have written, and the stories you had wanted to tell. Your children, your grandchildren, and your great-grandchildren miss you so much.

Chapter 1

I woke up with the sun as a resuscitated female asylum seeker. It was seven o'clock in the morning here in Italy—the land my late Gambian friend, Fatoumatta, once told was filled with milk and honey. I just took my meagre diet of bread and water. There was no glee on my face like I saw on other migrants who made the journey before me, but the experience on paths to Europe binds us together. Nine of us started the journey, but I was the only one that made it to Europe. Even though I was abducted as a slave—a modernized sex slave in Libya—lost my virginity and became pregnant before I could make it to Europe, I survived. I could still feel the manacles around my ankles and handcuffs around my hands like a criminal.

I'm not nervous or reticent to tell my story. I ran away from what I thought was a cub and faced its fierce mother. I was left with no choice but to face it violently. My dream to dine in sumptuous environs was not fulfilled.

I died many times on the way: in the desert in Mali, at the hands of my adductors in Libya, and in the Mediterranean Sea. The day we faced the devilish sea, hundreds of migrants died and never came back to life. Yes, I was one of those that used the deadliest migration route in the world to get here; my conscience continued to prick me every day. Many made death their only hope because it was seen as the only rescuer.

Frankly speaking, my Gambian friend, Fatoumatta, hid the truth about the danger that was ahead of us until when we were finally on board the boat. She then told me she had made the journey at her peril. I take responsibility for the trials and tribulations I went through. It is life and death in the Mediterranean. I saw what death and survival looked like with numerous corpses floating on the water.

I missed my family, my friends in Sierra Leone, and the gorgeous people I met in my struggle to Europe. I missed the people we started the dangerous journey together. Fatoumatta, a Gambian, who was as well sold as a sex slave with others and later drowned in the sea. Sabel, a Gambian, died of complications in Agadez, Mali. Grace, a Nigerian, was gang-raped somewhere in the Sahara Desert. Alberta, a Liberian, was killed together with Sainabou while they were trying to escape the tyrannies of our adductors. Sulay, a Sierra Leonean, happened to be the second person that died amongst us—he never saw the rising sun in Mali. Awa, a Gambian, died in Senegal before we even departed—she was the first amongst us to die. Martin, a Bissau-Guinean, was stabbed multiple times as we got closer to the Malian border with Algeria. Sainabou, a Gambian, was killed at the side of Alberta.

To Jadati and her grandson who picked me up when I was dumped half-dead in the wilderness. I could remember the precious words of hope from them, the reasons that prompted their desperations to cross the mighty sea, and the pains that pushed us could only be felt by us. Some called our reason poverty, some called it shame, some called it desperation, some called it laziness, faithlessness, and hopelessness, all was nonsense and baseless…blah blah. If you ask any of us that made it to Europe, we will tell you about the unrecognized lives we once lived; we will miserably talk about life as a slave in our home country—how we were pushed to be swallowed by a hungry sea because our identities were considered curses to our struggling nations. You would hear us speaking about how we hopelessly waited for the dehumanized laws to change in everyone's favour. We were all tired of babysitting our miseries in our various countries.

My heart goes to the elegant folks we met on the way, like Emmanuel and Franck from Ivory Coast and Ahmed from Mali. They stood for us—especially Ahmed, who died trying to protect us. Getting to Europe, through Libya the major gateway was hell, but I will try to tell you my own story.

One of the inescapable facts is that not all migrants who left their countries made it to Europe; many perished before they got to Libya and are still dying on the way. And all those who made it, did it with unvarnished scars in their lives. Our experiences scarred us for life.

To the many repeated questions that I have received from my European friends on whether my decision still gratifies me: yes, I am super proud—extremely pleased. Had I not joined the group, who would have told the story of the other night? Had I not made this voyage, a delicate part of my body would have been mutilated by some folks trying to honour the desires of their foremothers who didn't understand the damage behind it.

And to the other repetitive question I received even yesterday, whether I should encourage others to make the same journey: No!

Hell no! There is no possibility you are going to make it. Those who have died surpass those that are here. When I fell into the sea, I had no option but to swim or I drown.

Next to the other boring question I have been asked was how I feel whenever I see the child that I got during the journey. I feel proud of myself for being a mother to a beautiful girl. Reminiscing how I got the pregnancy is painful. Yes, I reviled myself for getting pregnant by my adductors. Yes, I had the wish to abort her. Yes, I hated myself for a very long time. And yes, I was ashamed of myself, because I felt it ruined my whole life. But life, on its own, gives us choices to make. I had the option to terminate my baby's life forever and live with the destructive memory or welcome a positive contributor to earth to share my reminiscences. The gospel truth is the only alternative was to abort the baby and die with it.

I am a Sierra Leonean named Mattia—the only child to the late Brima Swarray and Kadiatu Conteh. I was not fortunate to see my parents in flesh, only in pictures. Yes, I was orphaned by the war. I was told my father was a soldier, who was wounded in action—he died of pains and depression when I was five months in my mother's womb. After thirty years of service in the military, he lost his right leg and had brain damage; he was appreciated with six million Leones {$1,000 at that time}. I called it an appreciation, not compensation to someone who was amputated and served his country for over two decades.

About a week ago, my Italian friend told me she was making around 1,700 euros a month, which was two times my father's so-called benefit. Perhaps it was the same agony that led to my mother's death, just a few hours after I was born.

It could be! It's so weird for a single parent to raise a child, especially there in Africa—an acute difficulty most women can't stand. I lost the note left behind by my father—a just man, I think. In his letter, I memorized the last sentence, which is so precious to me. "I'm glad I served my country and my conscience diligently." He didn't mention anything about his parents or his hometown but wrote about his frustration with the government of Sierra Leone. His childhood friend and squad mate, Warrant Officer Class Two, James Bangura, told me much about him when we met at the Wilberforce Barracks football field. (His astute daughter happens to be my friend, so she invited me to her school's annual sports meeting.)

Before I arrived at the school, his daughter, Mariatu Bangura, had already told him about me. With his baritone voice, He asked me who my father was. I told him I'd never met my father, but I was told his name was Brima Swarray. He was shocked because he never knew my father to be a father. "The late ex-serviceman?" he asked me again with more curiosity. He was the first person who showed me a picture of my dad in a military uniform.

My mother lost her parents during the eleven years of brutal civil war, which left my country with zilch to be proud of. She left Makeni with two of her bosom friends, Aunty Mabinty (with her daughter Zainab) and Aunty Sallay. She travelled to Freetown, the capital city of Sierra Leone, on the 30th of December 1998. A week later, the city was under attack by the RUF rebels, and my mother was gang-raped. Aunty Sallay was shot and killed by a stray bullet. Aunty Mabinty told me all this. I wish she were still alive; I would have confirmed from her many things I know not about my beloved mum.

I was born on the 17th of November 2002, the very day late President Ahmed Tejan Kabba declared Sierra Leone a conflict-free country. Since mama gave up the ghost a few hours after my birth, Aunty Mabinty, a very dutiful woman, became my foster parent. She was a nursery nurse. I grew up knowing her as my mother, and Zainab as my sister. Even though I wasn't fortunate enough to go to nursery school, I could sing a lot of nursery rhymes—things I learned through the horrible voice of Aunty Mabinty. Skinny Zainab was six years older than me, but we were of the same height and body size. Aunty Mabinty was that type of woman who never got bored with me, even though I used to talk a lot. Sometimes I used to ask her if she wanted to be alone because I didn't want to be seen as a nuisance.

Aunty Mabinty's husband, Uncle Hassan, isn't Zainab's father. At first, we both thought he was our father, until one day Zainab and I heard him telling his friend he was tired of taking care of other people's children. "I can't continue to take care of dogs for government. I want God to give me mine now!" We never believed what we heard until he repeated the same sentence in front of us one evening when Aunty Mabinty returned home. She turned sharply, gazed at Uncle Hassan, and then quietly ambled into her bedroom. We didn't see her until the following morning. We noticed it was not something she wanted us to know; probably, it was said at the wrong time, at the wrong place. We tried two times to confront her with questions regarding our natural parents, but in the mornings, she was always in haste to leave the house, and she would come back home in the evening weary. With compassion, we tried not to make her weak at the knees with our questions.

One Saturday, she took us to the Aberdeen Beach and told us the truth about my parents and Zainab's father. Zainab's biological father was a polygamous, superbly wealthy diamond dealer killed by rebels in the Kono district, and a man who didn't respect women— probably because of six wives and countless concubines. In the Poda Poda {minivan}, Aunty Mabinty sensed from our faces the effect of what she told us. She told us to act normal before we got home.

Uncle Hassan was in the sitting room, drinking a bracer— something Aunty Mabinty always frowned at. My aunty, or Zainab's mother, used to tuck us to sleep—even when Zainab was sixteen years old, and I was ten—but not on that day.

On Sundays, we used to go to church with Aunty Mabinty, a devout born-again Christian, and on Fridays, we would go to the Mosque with Uncle Hassan, a fervent believer in Islam. It came to the time when they both abandoned the church and Mosque with excuses we couldn't comprehend. Agreeing to differ, Uncle Hassan said he didn't see anything that could prove God existed, and Aunty Mabinty told us God would hear her when she prayed from home. "God's everywhere," she would say and smile. I agonized for weeks over whether I should be a Christian or a Muslim, but I ended up being an agnostic human being; it didn't stop me from reading both the Bible and the Koran on our bedside table.

The following day, around six o'clock—which was her usual time to leave home—Aunty checked on us to see whether we had returned to normality and had prepared for schooling. My eyes were open, Zainab was busy snoring, and without a word to me, she shut the door and left the house.

Many times, Aunty Mabinty and Uncle Hassan had confrontations—not because of us, nor his irritating statements, but his habit of looking at pornographic magazines and intentionally leaving them in the sitting room. So, trying to keep our content, at the same time trying to protect his nuptial ecstasy, was a bit difficult for Aunty. Not once, not twice, in their living room, we overheard Aunty Mabinty pleading with him to stop bringing such things home. "We have children here, and they are girls!" His usual response would be, "Does that mean I should deprive myself?" All of us have gotten used to Uncle's vitriol. Aunty Mabinty didn't like filtering away money, but her wastrel husband—a womanizer, a night watchman— didn't see money as a valuable object. Uncle Hassan was nice whenever he received his salary, but then again unwatchable when his money ran out.

One day, we were watching a popular comedy show on TV called 'Wan Pot' on the Sierra Leone Broadcasting Service. They got to a scene where a female impersonator, Rosaline, was caught with a boyfriend. Uncle Hassan chuckled and giggled loudly for about thirty seconds. With his normal frivolities, we took notice that he was drunk again that night. Aunty Mabinty nudged my left hand and blinked her left eye. I was expecting her nudging—even Zainab too, I am sure. Besides what happened that night, Aunty Mabinty would nudge us or blink her eyes if she wanted to talk to a visitor in private or to her husband. On that night, we were so reluctant to leave the sitting room at first, because the comic play was very interesting, but the way Aunty glared at us made us nervous, so we left unwillingly.

On Saturdays, we joined Aunty downtown to assist her in running the kitchen utensils business, which she started a few years after my birth. One unfortunate Saturday for Uncle Hassan, Aunty Mabinty went home and caught him seducing the maid. The following day, the twenty-four-year-old maid was sent back to her village. Aunty kept us in the dark until about three days after our neighbour's daughter, who overheard the tussling, gave us a clue about what happened in our absence. Zainab and I were wondering what prompted Aunty's action, with all the beautiful things she had said about the maid. Since that day, Aunty kept more watchful eyes on us.

A month to the end of the academic year 2012—I was nine, going to ten years old—and I just took my National Primary School examination. Zainab was sixteen years nymphet, getting ready to face the West Africa Senior School Certificate examination. Aunty Mabinty took us again to Aberdeen Beach where she disclosed to us that she would be sending us away to our relatives. "Why, Mama?" Sadly, Zainab asked her. It was the first time Zainab had called her mama. I never called her such a name; we heard people calling her Aunty since we were babies. Aunty tried not to look at our disappointed faces. "I've nurtured you guys since birth in that environment, but it's high time you change location and gain new experiences. Your aunty, with whom you are going to stay, is a very nice woman too." She expected us to respond, but not a single word came out of our mouths. Zainab nuzzled up against me when she noticed the change in my emotion. "I love you guys, and I want the very best for you," Aunty commented again. No response again from us. She finally put it in a nutshell. "My home is no longer safe for you girls." We nodded our heads. She knew we weren't happy but had no other alternative.

That night, as we lay on our beds, we both cried bitterly in silence, afraid to miss the good parenting of Aunty Mabinty. Nobody came to console us. No one else knew.

The next morning, Aunty Mabinty told us she had changed our daily route. Instead of going home directly after school, we should join her at the marketplace. We obeyed and never complained. I thought she needed us there to assist; she would instead ask us to read our books in a noisy and congested community.

Next to her was a very funny shoemaker, a male friend to my aunty by the name of Ansumana Kuhpoa, born and raised in Makeni, fluent in both the two giant languages in Sierra Leone—Mende and Temne. To attract customers, he would sing from morning to evening. He was the first person that proudly told me he was trying to raise funds to cross the Mediterranean Sea, calling Africa an abyss on earth.

The first day we joined Aunty immediately after school, we were very bushed and worn out. I wanted to take a nap, but only a toddler could sleep in such an environment, so I decided to sit by Ansumana, the shoemaker. I dug him with a statement to get his attention. "Frankly, I thought you were a runaway culprit." He just hissed at me and smiled.

I asked him, "Do you want to cross the sea?"

"Of course! Why shouldn't I?" he responded.

"Ansumana, can't you see thousands of people die crossing that sea every day, huh?" I asked him again.

He smiled and said, "I know you are a fan of the media. Don't believe everything they say; forget the media! It's their job to discourage us from making the journey. Every day, the politicians are giving us more reasons to die in the sea. Can't you see the situation is getting worse every single minute? They are not talking about the unpleasant life potential youths like us are living, because they have been paid by politicians to act like they are visually impaired." Then he continued whistling. Turning towards me again, he said, "My late father was a rich and foolish gold miner, and he lavished all his money on women and abandoned my sick mother in Kabala. He died with not even a teaspoon left behind to be proud of—absolutely no foundation to stand on! I had to drop out of school to provide for my sick mum. So, I've two options now. Either I get the money required to give her good medication for the rest of her life, or I die trying. God knows I have tried!" His eyes became red; pain was written all over his face. I got his message and left his presence.

I left Ansumana and went to a gaily salon to cut my hair short at the nape of my neck. While waiting to be attended to, some ladies were expressing their frustrations regarding Sierra Leone's economy, and the issue about the sea crossing came up; then the parlour went silent.

A very beautiful lady with gadgets in her hands heavily denounced the idea, and the two ladies I sat next to on a long wooden bench murmured. "It's a choice for a woman not to suffer anywhere in the world because God gave us something we can use to survive," the lady said and smiled. Her comments went with some gales of laughter, but the owner of the salon, Aunty Salome—a kind elderly friend to me—responded to the lady, "Be mindful of your statement, dear; we have a young, innocent girl sitting with us."

"It's just a gag!" the lady responded to the hairdresser and smiled again. She turned and said to me, "Don't mind my one-liner, please. Darling, it's a girls' thing."

From the look on Aunty Salome's face, I knew she wasn't happy with the lady's joke. Not too long after, another lady received a phone call. Her friend's younger brother, who tried to make the journey, was shot dead by some militia in Libya. She immediately left the salon in a very depressed mood. The Mediterranean Sea crossing is nicknamed "Temple Run," a name common among youths around downtown Freetown. When I returned to my aunt, they were already waiting for me to go home.

On board the minibus, Aunty Mabinty deterred us from spending time in the sitting room until she moved us out of the house; the comfort of the room was no longer available to us. I felt hemmed by the restrictions in the house. When we got home, inside our untidy room, I blub in my heart, why should we be deprived? I was madly in love with the 'Wan Pot' show that aired every Saturday. Not too long after, we heard Uncle Hassan hurling insults at Aunty Mabinty in their bedroom, but Aunty didn't throw any word at him. My hunger for knowledge made me forget that soon, and I read my books.

In the still of the night, I woke and saw Zainab looking at one of Uncle Hassan's pornographic books. I gazed at her aghast—couldn't believe what my eyes saw. She threatened to hate and distance me if I ever disclosed it to anyone. I had the intention to tell Aunty; then again, Zainab was my closest buddy, and I didn't want her to see me as an enemy.

The next day, Zainab passed by my school and persuaded me to spend all the money given to us by my aunt to cover our lunch and transportation. We had to walk from St. John to Malama Thomas Street; both my legs hurt me so badly. Zainab again warned me not to tell Aunty Mabinty.

Later, Aunty started asking me tricky questions to know why my bitter face. I quickly left her presence and sat by Ansumana, who was busy attending to customers—one of them a lunatic man, who was very conscious of wearing slippers on an untidy outfit.

After attending to his customers, Ansumana turned towards me and said, "Please—I don't want to hear anything the media may have said about the Mediterranean Sea. Since the Europeans refused to come and share their wealth with us, we are going there to share our poverty with them. You are addicted to the media, aren't you?"

A frown formed on my face, and I didn't respond to him, mistaking his comment as a ferocious attack on me. Then I realized that was just him.

"Ngor Miatta!" He shouted my name. I always smiled when he called my name like that. Ngor means "elder brother/sister" in the Mende dialect.

"You're like a brother to me. I don't want to lose you," I responded to him.

"Thank you!" he said and focused on his work. As he was sewing, he said to me, "Since you hate losing me, what have you gained by seeing me in total destitute? Some would be successful through education, some through God's given gift, but I and many others would be successful through crossing that giant sea. There are many ways to the top of the mountain, but only one view." He said something in Temne that I couldn't understand, and he refused to interpret it for me.

"But yours is a meteoric rise to success," I said.

"If I go through the natural process, my mum would've been dead, and if she dies, I would be a big fool," he commented.

When we got home that evening, to our surprise, we met Uncle Hassan. He always leaves home by 6 p.m. and goes to the east end of Freetown to work. We met him at home again the following day, whistling and mincing up and down. Zainab and I were wondering why. He probably disclosed the reason to his wife, and they decided to keep us in the dark. Zainab had the feeling that Uncle Hassan was seeing us as implacable foes, accusing us of disclosing his secret relationship with the maid to his wife.

The following morning, Aunty immediately left for the market. As we were preparing to go to school, we overheard Uncle Hassan talking to Uncle Issa, his bosom friend, asking him to assist him with millions of Leones to make a journey to Europe—the scariest thing in the world to me even to this day. Zainab elbowed me to pay great attention to their phone conversation.

As we were returning home in the evening with Aunty, walking towards the bus station, she told us we shouldn't mind our uncle. "He was asking for millions to die in the sea, and he swims like stone," she said, and we laughed.

"What about his job?" Zainab asked her with curiosity when we were on board the bus.

"He has been sacked for no reason!" Aunty replied. Zainab and I gazed at each other, and the men sitting next to us smiled. "Yeah, that's what he told me," she continued.

A few days later, he became a milliner in Freetown, standing around Lightfoot Boston Street by Poultney Street—a popular area called Belgium.

For the very first time, Zainab told me about her boyfriend, who was also a peddler around that same locality. She said the boy was a high school dropout, fair and handsome. She warned me again not to tell Aunty.

About a week later, at my third term examinations, news came to Aunty that the woman she wanted us to stay with couldn't accommodate us both, which became a millstone around her neck. It took days before she revealed it to us. "Now, Zainab, you're going to stay with her, because your external exam is at your doorstep. Miatta, you shall move to Bo Town and stay with another friend of mine, since you've taken your exams. She was also a great friend to your late mum. I will be sending you guys everything that you need, so don't worry!" Aunty Mabinty said to us.

The revelation spoilt my day. Having nothing to say, I left her presence and went straight to my room. "How can I move to a place I have never been, or stay with someone I have never met, with no one around me that I've known before? Is she trying to separate me from Zainab because I wasn't her biological daughter, or winnow out of her family?" I asked myself all those questions as I lay on my bed that night. I had a sleepless night.

I was reluctant to go with Aunty to the market, but she insisted I go with her, so we went. I helped her pack her stuff by the roadside, and then I sat next to her wistfully for hours. Ansumana called me Ngor Miatta. I gave him a wintry smile. He called again, but I ignored him. Zainab arrived from school immediately, and Aunty asked her to look after the stuff. She took me to a beautiful restaurant around Wilberforce Street and had a one-on-one chat with me.

"Before your mother, Kadiatu, died, I promised to take good care of you and love you as my daughter. Protecting you is my priority, and from what I've seen and heard in my husband's house, it's no longer safe for girls. You have been with me for a great many years; it would be a complete wipe-out to me if I let anything bad happen to you. Just know that I'm not sending you away from me forever. Within one year, I would have figured out the best solution. This is the oddest decision I'm taking in my life, but it's for your betterment," she said. She grabbed me, and I watched her shed tears.

The palatable food she bought was left there untouched. I had to pretend like I acknowledged all that she said to please my soul. What she told me at that restaurant wasn't convincing to me.

We joined Zainab about an hour later. I tried to contemplate so I could agree with myself. I tried to stay awake all night, reading through Aunty Mabinty's words, but couldn't come up with anything better but bitterness to my soul. "They want to desert me," was the mantra in my head. As I was fighting with my thoughts, I remembered the pornographic book I caught Zainab looking at the other night. I searched for it that night like a missing diamond, but I could not find it. Zainab woke up quietly and caught me moving helter skelter inside the room. "What are you looking for?" she asked.

"I'm looking for the pornographic book, of course," I responded.

"Huh! Why?" she asked me.

"I don't know!" I replied confidently.

"Miatta? Miatta? I've noticed lately you are looking for my trouble. Stop what you're doing!" She stretched her matchstick legs and went to sleep. After some time, I wanted to continue searching, but her eyelids wouldn't stop blinking. She couldn't continue pretending to be asleep, so she sat up and smiled. "If you were a witch, you would become popular in the underworld. Don't you think so?" she asked, and I shook my head and smiled.

Zainab was the first person to wake up at dawn. I knew she may have repositioned the book to a place that would be difficult for me or any other person to lay hands on. The room was where Aunty stored her goods, and at the same time it was a chamber to sleep. To my surprise, she left for school very early and joined us two hours late after school. Aunty interrogated her, but smart Zainab dodged all the questions asked. We both knew that wasn't our usual time of returning home. She whispered in my ear, telling me her boyfriend was traveling to Europe by way of the sea. I wanted to ask if she was talking about the Mediterranean Sea. As I pronounced the first three syllables of the word, she grabbed my mouth. "Are you crazy? Do you want Aunty to hear it?" she hissed at me.

I became silent and walked over to sit by Ansumana, though I knew he was a bit mad at me because of my naughty behaviour the other day. After talking on the phone, he said, "I knew you would come to me again one day; the mischievousness of children is natural, not taught, so adults should just ignore. Let me tell you about my mama's present situation before you start telling me about the distorted news from the media. She's presently in a very critical situation, which means I have to dig in, get money from my savings, and send it for her medication."

I had compassion for him, but I didn't show it. Instead, I took out my mathematics exam answer paper and showed it to him. He praised me and told me he flunked math many times.

Later, Zainab told me more about her boyfriend's plan to cross the sea. She said it as if it wasn't difficult and there were no obstacles in the way. It seems she had not seen or heard about the hundreds or thousands of Africans and other nationals dying every week. Not too long after she was explaining that to me, Aunty and Uncle invited Zainab to the backyard of the house. Even though I wasn't invited, I had to go. Uncle Hassan sat on a plastic chair, with a shaved head as big as Jupiter, a neat turtleneck sweater, and slippers; and Aunty Mabinty had her hair in a bun and wore a dressing gown with flip-flops on her feet. With the looks on the couple's faces, I knew something was wrong, so I started accusing myself of my thoughts.

"Zainab, how old are you now?" Aunty asked.

"I'm sixteen years," she replied.

"You're still a child, right?" Aunty asked her.

"Yes, Aunty," she answered.

"Okay, where were you when you left school yesterday?" Aunty asked.

Zainab didn't respond.

"What time did school close yesterday?" she again asked her.

"Noon, Aunty," Zainab answered.

"And when did you join us at the marketplace?" Aunty asked.

"Around 4:00 p.m., Aunty," Zainab responded.

"And who's Mustapha Marrah, or Nasty Bee, as he nicknamed himself?" Uncle Hassan, with his thunderous voice, interrupted Aunty and asked Zainab.

I was looking at Aunty when Uncle asked the question then glanced at Zainab. I'd never heard the name before—not even in my school. She clung to the frame of the door with her right hand while concentrating on the ceiling. I could sense her legs shivering and sweating.

Aunty stood up and said in a furious tone, "I don't even want to hear that ancient cliché from you. You left school early yesterday and spent time with the idiotic boyfriend of yours, Mustapha, and he has the guts to brag about it to your uncle, huh? You are barking up the wrong tree if you expect us to give you full support when you get pregnant at such a tender age! Can't you see the difficulties I am going through to give you the best education instead of being a fashionista like my friends? I made myself look like an old woman with old-fashioned dresses in this city just for you!"

I paid great attention to the barrage of questions from Aunty and the unflattering comments from Uncle, but I was soon found out. "Miatta, get back to your room!" Aunty ordered me.

Frankly, I felt bad. Oh yes, I did. I wanted to be there from the beginning to the very end. Right there, I was wondering how the so-called Mustapha and Uncle Hassan knew each other; how did they meet? Well, because they were both bargain hunters in the streets of Freetown. I know Aunty Mabinty's bark is worse than her bite. Uncle Hassan was just the same. He used to say children should learn by themselves; the rod won't help.

Zainab returned to our room forty-five minutes later, laid down, and started sniffling; she didn't say a word to me. I heard Uncle Hassan barracking in the sitting room as he was watching a soccer game on TV. I went out to the sitting room, hoping to find Aunty, who promised to give me two thousand Leones to buy local food, but I was too nervous to knock on her bedroom door, so I returned to my room and found Zainab had barricaded herself on the bed. She's not the type of human who can stay unflappable.

* * *

I was waiting unwillingly for a date to leave for Bo Town—the south of Sierra Leone—while Zainab waited to move to Lumley, the west end of Freetown. A week later, Aunty asked me to prepare. I was to leave the following week. I felt sick, weak and unfit to leave my aunt's presence.

The fixed date I was supposed to travel passed. I didn't bother to ask Aunty; my body and soul knew I hated to go. Another week came and passed, and after four weeks, Aunty told us we were going nowhere. We couldn't believe it, but I was more curious why she changed her mind after all the things she had said. She could not just change things inexplicably, even though I felt so relieved.

After her second visit to the hospital within a week, she disclosed to us she was pregnant. We congratulated and celebrated her until the following day; not because of her pregnancy, but because she was an industrious woman. Abandoning the idea of sending us away from her, she inducted us into running her business, as there would come a time that she would not be punctual. I had the opportunity to understand my aunty very well and know much about her and my late beloved mother, Kadiatu.

Chapter 2

Aunty Jestina—a very chubby, healthy woman with whom I was supposed to have moved with to Bo Town—visited us in Freetown. She was so concerned about hygiene I mistook her to be a nurse. It was only later Aunty Mabinty told me she was a barmaid.

In the sitting room, where we had been restricted by Aunty Mabinty, Aunty Jestina invited me there twice, but I was very adamant to obey her.

One day, Aunty Mabinty was out of the house to buy some vegetables for our visitor; she didn't like sending us out of the house after the sun set. Aunty Mabinty returned just as Aunty Jestina raised her voice in a terribly angry tone regarding us not joining her in the sitting room. I heard her telling our visitor she had prohibited us from spending time in the sitting room. Aunty Jestina didn't bother asking why; she knew Aunty Mabinty as an inflexible human, despite their cordiality.

A minute later, Aunty Jestina knocked at our door. "Come in, Aunty!" I said. She's a nice, pretty woman always with a smile on her face. As soon as she entered our room, I bowed my head, suddenly shy.

"You are such an intelligent girl. Have you received your NPSE result from the government?" she asked me with her right hand on my back. I shook my head with gentility. "I'm sure you will come out with flying colours. Do you believe that?"

"I do, Aunty," I responded.

"Your mum, Kadiatu, was a very special friend to me—so helpful, so humble like you. She did a lot for me when I was unwaged, and her unwavering support motivated me. She was my schoolmate; we both attended Holy Rosary Senior School," she told me. I raised my head and looked at her, and then I bowed it again. She was the first woman I saw with a bristle on her chin. I wanted to ask her a few questions about my mother's childhood life. I don't know whether I was afraid or shy.

"Are you shy with me?" she asked me.

Feeling braver, I smiled and asked her, "Do you have my mother's childhood picture?"

"No, sweetie, but she lives in my memory," she replied. I wanted to tell her I can't see her memory; it would have sounded so disrespectful to her.

"Why is it that nobody has her picture?" I asked her.

It took time for her to respond to my question. Rubbing her right palm on my left hand, she said, "I don't have it, but a friend of ours, who travelled as a refugee to the United States of America during our civil war, promised to mail a copy to me within this year."

I know my mother outlived my father by four months. I had critical questions to ask her, because she met my father on numerous occasions before he died, and going down that road is weird.

"Everybody says good things about her. Why then did God let her die?" I asked again when my head was bowed. She tried to look at my face, but I was unwilling to raise it. *Was my mother a bad person?* I asked myself in my mind. I thought about what our Sunday school teacher used to tell us: the only good person is the departed one. I constantly thought about my parents—the pains growing up without them—but the 'Wan Pot' comedians assisted me to unwind. Before Aunty Jestina left the room, she told me how unwise it is to question God. I didn't know she was fluent in British English until she received a call in my chamber—very much sounding like Aunty Mabinty.

Early in the morning, while we were still at home preparing to go to the market, Uncle Hassan unwontedly went out of the house at a brisk pace without even saying goodbye to his wife. Aunty Mabinty told Aunty Jestina she didn't know what her husband was up to. As we were walking to the bus station, I overheard Aunty Jestina telling Aunty Mabinty to start saving at the bank, not home, saving a huge amount of money at home is unsafe. In a very polite tone, Aunty Mabinty told her she trusted every single person at home. "Trust nobody and see everyone as a suspect. Besides all that, it's detrimental to keep an enormous amount in your house. I hate to sound pessimistic, Mabinty. Don't say you didn't know!" Aunty Jestina said.

"Thanks for your honest suggestion, Jestina. I will definitely think about it and know what to do," Aunty Mabinty responded.

When we get to the marketplace, not too long after, I heard Aunty Mabinty introducing Ansumana to Aunty Jestina in Mende. I was so surprised; I never heard or thought Aunty Mabinty could speak Mende. Ansumana is always courageous to talk about his struggle and the difficulties in taking care of his mum, and bold enough to tell people about his desire to cross the giant sea. I don't know why I was so interested to hear about it. I wasn't fluent in Mende, but at least nobody would plan my death in front of me.

After two days with us, Aunty Jestina returned to Bo Town, leaving a brand-new cell phone with me. I wasn't a novice in using it. I bought a sim card and reached out to her. She was terrifically happy to hear my melodious voice.

After a month and a half—highly expecting my result to be out, hoping to outperform my friend Haja, and thinking about my school of choice—Uncle Hassan disappeared from home. Aunty Mabinty tried to telephone him many times, but he was out of reach and nowhere to be seen. It was the summer holiday. She left Zainab to watch over the stuff and we went together and reported him missing to the police. The police promised to do their best to search for him. I sensed Aunty wasn't satisfied at all. Once we left the police station, she called several of Uncle's relatives but got a negative reply from them. She again phoned her own family members, who were not happy with her relationship with Uncle Hassan, and she was given the cold shoulder.

The third day, very early in the morning, Aunty Mabinty rushed out of her bedroom half-naked, shouting, "My money! My money!" Her eyes were very red like a hunting lioness. We stood gazing like fools, not knowing exactly what happened or what to do. Our neighbour, Aunty Erica, knocked at our front door; I'm sure she heard Aunty's voice. She was also surprised to see Aunty only partly dressed.

"What happened, Mabinty?" Aunty Erica asked.

Aunty kept crying and screaming, "My money! My money! Erica, my money!"

Aunty Erica asked us to leave their presence, so we went to our room. I started fighting with my thoughts again, which is something I do every day as an optimist. That day, I became a pessimist because I had never seen my sober-minded aunty in such a horrible mood.

Half an hour later, Aunty Erica called Zainab to shut the main door to the house, as they were going out. Zainab told me someone in the house may have stolen Aunty's savings, and we all knew the oppressive suspect. Two hours after they left, I took out the phone Aunty Jestina bought me and tried uncountable times calling Aunty. She didn't pick up my call.

Aunty Erica later called the house and told us they were at an outlying area of Freetown City, and Zainab—who understands the area much better, and has been there uncountable times—told me Uncle Hassan's family resides there.

The previous night, Zainab created a Facebook account for herself on my darling phone and taught me a few things. Oh, I love Facebook, and I always wanted to be online. I love staying online for hours; not like Zainab, who can outlast me.

Just after Zainab signed in, around 10 o'clock, we heard a heavy knock on the front door. It was Aunty Mabinty, Aunty Erica, and another strange woman. The looks on their faces made us shiver and too nervous to ask any questions. Not a word from even our aunty we had known to be our mother; not even a peck, as she always does. Aunty Erica asked us to lodge the strange woman in our room and let

Aunty Mabinty be. I tried, because I was a little bit scared of the stranger, so it seemed inevitable. I fell asleep and slept like a baby.

In the morning, as soon as I woke up, I saw the woman sitting on our study chair as she gazed at us. *Very observant,* I thought. Aunty Erica came to our house early in the morning to check on Aunty Mabinty, and the stranger whispered a few things in her ear. The appearance on Aunty Erica's face changed at once. I knew what the stranger said to her was outrageous. "Zainab, meet me outside!" Aunty Erica commanded. Three of them went outside the house with me alone in the sitting room. They didn't return to the house until about an hour later. They returned like cats, so quiet and discouraged. Zainab changed her girl's look. Aunty Erica's face faded away, not like the stranger's face which looked normal. I noticed something was wrong and weird; nobody could explain it to me. Is the stranger a sorceress? Is Zainab the suspect? My instinct is sometimes not frank with me, especially in a situation I am more concerned about. I felt terrified and lost.

Uncle Hassan's elder brother came to the house that morning to deliver a message from his brother. He confessed that Uncle Hassan stole the money, changed it to U.S. dollars, and then fled to Libya to cross the sea. He promised to pay it back when he made it to Europe. Unfortunately, he died of suffocation while crossing the dangerous desert a week after and Zainab was said to be one month pregnant. Aunty Mabinty collapsed and started bleeding profusely. She died before they arrived with her at the hospital.

It was a terror-stricken moment for us to know we have to live without our cherished Aunty Mabinty. I saw the whole situation as losing a mother twice. With the lugubrious expression on my face, I was able to smile briefly at my classmates and joked when they went to sympathize with my loss.

After her burial, we were sure to leave the house to stay with a responsible individual, or responsible individuals, as it happened. Sixteen-year-old Zainab, whose boyfriend died the same day with Uncle Hassan, should stay with Aunty Erica, a registered nurse. Aunty Jestina gently asked me if I could move with her to Bo. Well, I had no choice.

A guy who started the journey with Uncle Hassan called from Germany and informed us that my uncle had been buried in the desert at midnight, and the money found in his pocket was shared among them.

We left for Bo a week after the burial. At the bus station, which was very congested in the morning, we saw some strong youth, considered to be potential migrants, onboarding a bus to Guinea, Conakry. It was Aunty Jestina who made me take notice of them. I kept wondering how she knew about it and was able to identify them.

The police came by, looking for some muggers who had taken a considerable amount of money from a woman the previous day. They were informed that the criminals were loafers at the bus station. I was so surprised when Aunty called the nickname of one of the officers. They both hugged and smiled, and the cordiality was great through the expression on their faces. Aunty Jestina introduced the detective to me as her childhood friend and high school boyfriend, and the man happens to know my late mother, Kadiatu. The man was unwilling to acknowledge her statement, loath by Aunty to admit it. I wanted to ask him for a photo of my mother, but my garrulous aunty didn't let me, so I hauled my luggage onto the bus and put it in the luggage rack according to my ticket. It was inside the bus that she told me she depends on the alimony from her ex-husband, a lucrative businessman, and her salary as a barmaid. Her tuneful voice told me very beautiful stories about my mother that lulled me to sleep before we even left the Freetown municipality.

I woke up with tears in my eyes when we got to Moyamba Junction around noon. The bus parked for a thirty-minute break. I rushed out of the bus when I saw one of Aunty Mabinty's generous customers walking toward a restaurant. I shouted his name and hugged him.

"Mattia, what are you doing here?" he asked me.

"I'm moving to Bo Town with my other aunty," I responded.

"So, Mabinty allowed you to leave her presence?" he asked. I immediately realized he was unaware of my aunty's death.

"Aunty Mabinty has no choice," I replied.

"What do you mean?" he asked.

"Because she's dead!" Aunty Jestina interrupted us.

"What! When?" he asked.

"About two weekss ago," Aunty Jestina answered.

"I was planning to give her a call tonight. My fiancée is finally moving in with me, so I needed some kitchen utensils from her," he said as he knelt to look at my face. I can't stand the tears whenever I hear the good side about my cherished aunty. His eyes became blood red; he took out a handkerchief from his right pocket and wiped his face. I received a hug from him, a word of sympathy, and some money. He gave his phone number to Aunty to call him if she ran into any financial difficulty taking care of me.

I went back to the bus, and Aunty strolled with a waddling to one of the food vendors. She sent airtime to my phone and bought some vegetables and fruits to console me, which I saw as a weak-kneed appeaser. My late aunt's memory can't be wiped away. I missed my aunty so much.

I had never been to the provinces; that day was the first. We arrived in Bo at exactly 1:30 p.m. The sun was intensely hot. I checked my old electronic water resistance watch again to confirm the time. I still have the watch here with me. It's one of the assets that left with me after crossing the big sea, so I treasure it like a diamond.

Aunty Jestina hired two motorbikes that took us to an area called Shemigo, where Aunty's bar is located. At the back yard of the bar were two fat men and two beautiful ladies, sitting on their laps with anklets around their ankles. I gazed at their man-boobs for some seconds. It was the first time in my life to be around such environ; Aunty Mabinty prohibited us from being around any kind. Before we sat down, the men laughed over a black mamba killed outside the bar, while Aunty became furious and bounced on the cleaner for leaving the vicinity very untidy. "When an environment is dirty, it invites filthy creatures. Go and call Musa immediately to come and get this compound tidied up." I understood straight up that she was the manageress.

A few hours later, she took me to a community called Manjama, which was not too far from her bar. We went back to the bar after I took a nap and stayed there until midnight as I watched the waitresses serve guests. Never in my life had I stayed awake until midnight, so I slept til' 8 o'clock in the morning. The news about migrants dying again was all over the mainstream media, and in the street of Bo Town. Aunty called me a mummy's girl, and then I grinned. I knew it didn't go down with her.

I wanted to help the other girls in the kitchen; however, she asked me to cling to her and advance my managerial experience which I gained from Aunty Mabinty. Each day, she would call me to sit around her as she checked the expenditures made and the income that goes in. She is an expatriate in running bars and restaurants. Sometimes I would ask her to expand on something I couldn't understand.

There's a vast expanse at the back of the bar with mango and orange trees where customers relax during the day, especially when the sun is burning.

I was told Zainab was sick at the trimester of her pregnancy, and I was able to talk directly with her.

One day, a very fat man came to the bar, and Aunty Jestina introduced him as her boyfriend. He's a retired major of the Armed Forces of Sierra Leone. I wanted to ask him if he knew my father, after he offered me a drink at his expense, but I became nervous at the end. I waited for what seemed like years with my expectant face. I never saw him again until I left Africa. I was always in touch with Zainab and Aunty Erica in Freetown, and I have telephoned them several times since I arrived in Europe.

After that summer holiday, I started attending school. I never thought how life would be without my late aunt; I never stopped mourning for her in my quiet time. Even though Aunty Jestina is so caring—never should I compare her to Aunty Mabinty, the woman after my own heart—she would give me a huge amount of money to count. With a single mistake, I would start anew; an unforgeable moment with her. Why do angels never last long?

Within six months in Bo Town, I was inspired by Aunty Jestina's waitress to connect with old and new friends on Facebook. I was eleven years old, but Aunty's waitress suggested I change my date of birth to fifteen years, otherwise I would be rejected. After that, I received five friend requests from five boys in my community just five minutes once my account was activated. The waitress, with her angelic voice, told me to upload some nice photos of mine, which I also did. Ten more friend requests arrived that night, with one from a Gambian lady named Ya Rohey Jammeh. I accepted her friend request right away, thinking she was related to President Yayah Jammeh. With little understanding, I continued accepting friend requests without considering checking their profiles. Because of my strong admiration for England and English people, I figured out original English female names and added them. Within three days, my account was blocked. I created another account again a week later with little change in my information. My account was blocked after I sent twenty friend requests to some females from England again. I only created another Facebook account after six months, believing the system may have deleted my information. My new friend in school, who is a social media addict, advised me to stop sending friend requests to people I didn't know. Respectfully, I took her advice and went on to create another account, which I am now using here in Europe.

From the last account I created is where I met my friend, Fatoumatta Camara, who inspired me to make the deadliest journey. The conversation started with her surname, which is spelled Kamara in Sierra Leone. We had a lengthy discussion every day for over some weeks before we finally shared our personal phone numbers. She couldn't pronounce my name well, so I anglicised my name from Miatta to Martha. She told me about her former schoolmate named Martha.

"Are you a Muslim?" she asked me over the phone.

I answered, "No."

"Are you a Christian?" she asked me again.

"Hell no!" I replied.

"Should I ask if you're a Jew?" she asked with a laugh, and I did too. "Who are you then?"

"I'm a child of God," I replied.

"You're a Christian then, aren't you?" she suggested.

I made some comments to drag her from religion. Fatoumatta's father was a Gambian from the Mandingo tribe, and her mother was a Senegalese from the Wollof tribe. She was fluent in English, French, Mandinka, Wollof and a few local dialects. After six months in our friendship, at the end of my grade seven academic years, I told her my real age. "It doesn't matter your age. The fact is that you are real. There are a lot of fake people on social media lately," she said to me. While I am immune to expensive jokes, Fatoumatta was not; she would say funny jokes that could hurt me. I noticed she wasn't resistant to distress.

Aunty Jestina and I were talking under a mango tree at the back of the bar one day. She asked me whether I have been opportune to go through the Bondo Society. I shook my head. "Really? So, Mabinty never gave you the chance to learn about womanhood? That's unfair!" she said.

"Aunty, I don't want it. I can learn about womanhood through education," I said without fear on my face.

"It's not debatable! Just prepare yourself." She made the comment and left my presence.

I went straight to my room and had quiet time with myself. From that very moment, I developed doubt of everything I heard and saw in her house. I became very careful and planned to escape anywhere in Sierra Leone or out if she tried it. As a woman of her word, with an immutable heart, she continued to remind me about the preparation she was putting in place to get me initiated. My preparation was to run away from her house. Everyone in the house had gone through it and my friends in school too, so I had no pleasure discussing it with anyone.

When I went online to chat, I received a forwarded message from Fatoumatta, a story about an imp and a ghost. I couldn't read it to the end. While drinking an impala soup in the evening, I waited patiently online for over two hours, hoping to chat with her. At night, when Maria, my bed mate, returned home from the bar, she congratulated me in advance for going through the Bondo Society. I just smiled and laid down. I thought about it the whole night and became worried and heartbroken.

During summer school, Aunty told me the initiation was going to take place at Sembehu Town immediately after school closes for the first term holiday. The information from her inspired me more to run away. The question was, to whom? I tried very hard not to wear my heart on my sleeve, but my initiation wasn't a secret at all among the girls at home—probably even to other women and girls outside our house. Aunty was a person of popularity, influence, and wealth in our community, so running away from her was a difficulty for me.

I caught Fatoumatta online one afternoon just after I returned home from summer school, and I asked her a lot of questions, including her next step.

"How old are you now?" she asked me.

"I am eleven years, for now, my friend," I replied. We then talked for awhile about my situation.

Later, Aunty Jestina's fiancé, Uncle Julius Kpaka, arrived from the United States, and they were married within the first three weeks in Africa. Uncle Julius was a nice and interesting man, and I became accustomed to his witticism within his one month of stay in Sierra Leone. He called me Mama Miatta because his late mother's name was Miatta.

At first, I saw him as someone I could trust to help change his wife's mind. He promised me that he would send some money and other stuff to be used on my Bondo graduation day. I'm sure he knew I wasn't excited about his promises. I strived to show my dislike for the Bondo Female Society to both my aunt and uncle; they always gave me cold shoulders.

I became lazy in all that I did when I started seeing the magnitude of the challenges ahead of me, and all I could think about was how to escape…and the question again, to whom?

As the time drew near, day by day, I started having lengthy conversations on WhatsApp with my friend Fatoumatta. She told me about the lucrative job she had gotten in the tourism industry. She said, "Martha, if you have time, come and visit me in the Gambia."

I paused for a moment. That was exactly the gesture that I needed to escape such a devaluing of my womanhood.

"Martha, are you there?" she asked me.

"Yes, I am here, Fatou," I replied.

"I'm not a bad person. Don't worry, if you come here, I won't hurt you. So many of your fellow citizens are here," she said calmly.

I finally told her going to her country is expensive, and I can't afford the money…and also scary because I have never made such a journey.

"Just find out the cost and I will remit the money to you," she responded. I gave her the okay. It took me almost a week to execute the task.

The day I went to the bus station to make an inquiry, I saw two of Aunty Jestina's chief customers standing in front of the main building. They were bus drivers, too, driving from Bo Town to Freetown. I waited for hours for them to disappear, but unfortunately, none of them did, so I went back home. Fatou asked me again whether I was able to find out the cost. I paused and said, "I tried, but something came up, so I had to return home immediately."

I went straight to the bus station the next day after school, knowing that Aunty's customers wouldn't be there. I was interrogated by two other men, asking why I was leaving without an elderly person. Who was I going to see? And who was going to honour the bills? A fight erupted between two female passengers near to where me and the two men stood. The men left my presence to separate the ladies from the other side of the corner. A woman with a trinket around her neck, who was listening to our conversation, called me over and said, "My name is Kadiatu Sesay! What's your name, my daughter?"

I paused. "I am Miatta. You and my mother have the same name."

"Where's your mother?" she asked me. I became quiet. "My daughter!" she called my attention.

"I don't know where she is!" I replied to her.

"Huh! How is that possible?" she asked. Then she asked me to sit next to her. When she asked me again why I wanted to leave Sierra Leone, I told her life had become very unpleasant in my aunty's house. "Do you know anyone in the Gambia?" she asked me.

"Yes, ma'am, I do!" I replied.

"Do you have the money to pay?"

I told her my friend in the Gambia was ready to foot the bills.

"Do you know the approximate amount you need to get there?"

I told her again that was the reason I was there. She gave me all the details I needed to know and asked me to meet her when I was fully ready. She was a merchant, buying and selling stuff from Sierra Leone to the Gambia. Before I left the bus station, she requested contact details of Fatoumatta and my cell phone number.

When I left, I passed by Aunty's bar to collect the keys to the house. I was told Aunty was at home, worrying about me. I quietly entered my room when I got home, changed, and joined Aunty outside.

"Where have you been since the school closed today?" Aunty asked me.

I mistakenly replied to her, "I was at the bus station."

"To do what?" she anxiously asked me. I became speechless. "Have you started dating?" she teased me. I gave her a toothy smile. "Then tell me where you have been!"

I lied to her because I had no option. Everything concerning Bondo Society is trivial to me. I bashed at the waitress later that day when she tried to tell me the preparation Aunty was putting in place for my initiation graduation day. Aunty offered me a tripe soup triplicate, and I rejected it. She didn't bother asking me why. It was no longer hidden that I was seeing the secret society as an obstacle. These are some of the things I miss about nearest and dearest Aunty Mabinty, a respecter of no cruel cultures and traditions. Many a time, she expressed her displeasure at having gone through it. I told Aunty Jestina all that, and her reply was, "Aunty Mabinty was a born-again Christian from those Pentecostal churches. She also went through it, which made her a better woman before she died."

In the still of the night, I passed on the information to my friend Fatoumatta, who promised to forward the money within two days. I battled with my thoughts again the entire night: whether I was making the right decision, whether I was more than a mischievous child.

In the morning, before going to school, Aunty Jestina showed me the beautiful materials she had bought for the ceremony, and the money sent by her husband, Uncle Julius Kpaka, which irked me so badly.

My neighbour's daughter—also my classmate—disclosed it to some of my friends in school, and they provoked me, calling me names that irritated me. They revelled in annoying me every day in school. It gave me more reasons to run away—more reasons to face the risks, more courage to make myself uncomfortable in the unseen dangers. I became uncomfortable on earth, and I asked myself, "Is society a necessary evil?"

Surprisingly, Aunty Kadiatu told me she had received some money from Fatoumatta. "Should I go ahead and buy the bus ticket?" she asked on the phone. Replying with yes or no was a bit difficult for me, so I hung on to the phone and switched it off. I tried not to turn it on until the next day. The spirit of boldness got me, and I told Aunty Kadiatu to go ahead, so she bought the ticket and asked me to go and collect it.

Aunty Jestina wasn't at home; she travelled to Freetown to collect her visa at the U.S. embassy. It was a great opportunity for me to escape. Aunty Kadiatu told me I had to wait until the bus company has the required passengers, which could take days or weeks.

Aunty Jestina returned from Freetown with joy and excitement on her face and started having repeated absences from home, preparing to leave for the U.S. Four days later, Aunty Kadiatu phoned me and said the Gambian borders were closed to all Sierra Leoneans due to the Ebola outbreak. I asked Fatoumatta and she confirmed it. I became worried until I was told the government had banned all public gatherings, then I felt calm again. Aunty Kadiatu told me not to worry; my money would be refunded.

So, the discussion about my initiation into the society eventually disappeared, which was a relief because I was almost repelled by it. With no sign of repentance, before Aunty Jestina left for the U.S., she promised to visit us after three years, and one of her purposes would be to get me initiated into womanhood, as she claimed. I felt relieved, even though not fully respite.

Chapter 3

Three years after the Ebola outbreak, I was still in communication with Aunty Kadiatu, who promised to refund my money when I was ready, and with Fatoumatta, who was a little disappointed at what happened and that I couldn't make it. I had no intention of travelling out of my beloved country if not because of honouring a cruel culture. Fatoumatta never asked for her money since I couldn't make it as planned, and I didn't bother Aunty Kadiatu, a woman I sometimes called Mama. I was told by Zainab that Ansumana eventually made it to Europe through crossing the sea, and he had called several times to talk with me. Not like in Aunty Mabinty's house where we were deterred not to sit in the sitting room. Then again, at Aunty Jestina's house I had the freedom, but time couldn't permit me.

On Sunday, the third day of September 2016, I received a call from Aunty Jestina, reminding me that she was going to Africa and telling me how prepared she was for the initiation. She was a woman who believed children learn by repetition, so she would say the same thing anytime she called. I became fed up with her calling. I sent a WhatsApp message to Fatoumatta, but she didn't reply to me until after three days, even though she was online.

"I would be happy to see you. My friends and I are planning a voyage that will change our lives," Fatoumatta told me.

I had no understanding about the voyage she talked about, and I was so desperate to leave before Aunty Jestina got back from the U.S. I tried calling Aunty Kadiatu numerous times within a week. I couldn't reach her until one day I went to the bus station myself and found her sleeping under a huge mango tree. So extremely happy to see me, she told me that some bad boys at the bus station stole her phone.

"Are you ready to travel now?" she asked me

"Yes ma'am!" I responded.

She graciously told me to meet her after a week. She wanted to replenish part of the money she used. I excitedly left her presence and delivered the message to Fatoumatta, who kept forwarding the piece about the Gambia general election; she was a die-heard supporter of one of the main opposition parties.

Aunty arrived from the U.S. on the eighteenth day of October as a respectable married woman, with a lot of wear for my graduation from the society bush, while I was clandestinely still planning my journey to the Gambia. When she was away, I was told she had a confrontation with some elders from her father's house; she's not a respecter of persons. On the second day of December 2016, Fatoumatta sent me a voice message, shouting excitingly that Adama Barrow, the candidate she was supporting, had won the election.

Aunty Jestina sent me to the market, and I used the opportunity to see Aunty Kadiatu at the bus station. She showed me the ticket she had bought for me and gave me the remaining balance to be used on the way. I was astonished when I realized we were to depart Bo

Town the eve our family should travel to the village for the initiation ceremony. I thought about Aunty Jestina defending the indefensible, and I was probably making a wrong verdict. I became sick because of fear of the unknown and the danger ahead of me. A day for my departure to Banjul, and two days for my family trip to the village, the fear became severe and hurtful.

The day finally came that I was supposed to leave Sierra Leone. Aunty Jestina asked me to be with her the whole of the day, as we were preparing to travel to the village. Aunty Kadiatu and Fatoumatta called me several times to remind me of the departure time. I wanted to tell them I couldn't make it, but I didn't want to blow the opportunity away. We were to depart Bo Town at 9 p.m., and at 8, I was still sitting with Aunty Jestina at the bar. I almost gave up the idea to run away just to please Aunty Jestina. About forty minutes to the departure time, Aunty Kadiatu called me again and asked, "My daughter, where are you now? The bus is fully loaded, and you are the only passenger that's not here yet. Are you on your way?" I hung up then switched off my phone. With consideration, I left Aunty Jestina's presence, went outside the bar, and took a motorbike home. I quickly emptied my school bag, collected the money—the remaining cash I received from Aunty Kadiatu—put on a pair of jean trousers—two pants I didn't bother to check whether they were clean—and quickly left the house. I took another motorbike to the bus station, arriving a few minutes later.

Aunty Kadiatu couldn't believe it when she saw me. "I almost sold your seat," she said furiously to me. Before I entered the bus, she introduced me to the driver and asked him to watch over me. I never switched on my phone until I crossed the border between

Sierra Leone and Guinea, which was then around 8 a.m. the following morning, then I bought another sim card and hard access to my WhatsApp.

The journey was tedious and discouraging because of the tons of checkpoints mounted by the Guinean and Senegalese police and immigration officials demanding money for which I still don't understand why they're paid.

We arrived at the Gambian border after four days drive. Commotion and distress were there, with foreigners and citizens hasting to leave the country. We were told President Jammeh had refused to step down. Some Sierra Leonean men urged the driver to move on. "We've seen more than that!" a passenger shouted. The driver was very courageous to move.

I sent a WhatsApp message to Fatoumatta, as she asked me to cross the border immediately while she was trying to leave the country with her friends.

"Can you meet us in Dakar?" she asked me.

"No, I can't!" I replied to her.

"Yes, you can," she said. "You can get another bus from Basse where you are right now, to Dakar. Just asked for a directive."

I wanted to step off the bus, but the driver refused. He said I shouldn't leave the bus until we get to Serrekunda as instructed by Aunty Kadiatu. I told Fatoumatta about the impossibility and how adamant the driver had been. Ten minutes later, I was trying to figure out how to escape. Fatoumatta texted me again to know whether I had crossed the border. It was chaotic, as everyone was going helter skelter, trying to leave the Gambia and crossing the border with Senegal. Some of the passengers left the bus to find a temporal shelter, some to get more information on the situation. The driver returned to us with discouraging news. "Lets be patient please. The immigration officers are focusing on those trying to cross over to Senegal."

"Do you have enough money with you?" Fatoumatta messaged me.

"Hell, no!" I replied.

"Okay, let me get back to you shortly!" she commented.

I left my seat and moved to the other side of the bus to have a clear view of people leaving the country while I was waiting for Fatoumatta's response. In that process, some sharp object gouged my left hand without me even noticing. A very observant woman sitting behind me brought it to my notice. The wound was deep, but my hand didn't bleed much, and the woman asked if I was healthy. "You have got a deep cut, but you are not bleeding much," she said to me. I smiled painfully. The woman removed the cloth around her neck and gave it to me to wrap around my hand. On the course, I got a message notification from Fatoumatta asking me to drop down the bus, buy a sim card from one of the telecommunication companies, fixed it and send the number to her; her former classmate would go and pick me up. Immediately, I tried to step out of the bus. I saw the bus driver running towards me; he was interrupted by another Sierra Leonean who was evacuating the Gambia. I quietly sneaked and ran away.

I followed Fatoumatta's decision, bought the sim card with the help of one Gambian man, fixed the sim, and sent the number to Fatoumatta. It seemed I was in the good grace of the inhabitants of the community.

The next day, I waited until 1 p.m. before Fatoumatta's friend called me. She first said "bonjour" and I replied hello.

"Oh! I thought you are a Senegalese. I'm Fatoumatta's friend. She told me you need help. Where are you presently?" she asked me. I gave the phone to a Nigerian businessman to direct her to me. We were not able to meet too long. She gave me a gracious smile and sweet hug.

"My name is Sabel. What is your name, again? Fatoumatta told me your name, but I can't remember," Sabel said to me.

"My name is Miatta, but Fatoumatta calls me Martha," I replied to her.

"Which country are you from?" she asked me.

"I'm from Sierra Leone," I responded.

"Salone?" Sabel asked and gave me her gracious smile again.

With a polite smile on my face, I asked her, "How did you know that name?"

"I grew up with Sierra Leonean refugees in the Gambia. We have thousands of them here." Sabel pointed over to the Gambia town over the border. That town is called Basse Santa Su. Because of tough restrictions from the Gambia government, they couldn't make it to Banjul and other cities, so they settled down here instead. Can you speak Kono?" she asked me, and I answered no! "We've many of them in Basse," Sabel commented. "Fatoumatta told me also you want to travel to Dakar, right?"

"Yes, I do!"

"We can't leave now; if you do, we won't get there until midnight, and it's horrible, right?" she asked.

"Yeah! Are you also traveling to Dakar with me?" I questioned her.

She gave me her kind smile again, then nodded her head.

"Then staying would be horrible too. Do you know anyone here?" I asked.

"I know everyone."

Sabel held on to my left hand and walked with me around the border town. On our way to nowhere, we got to a food vendor and stood there. While Sabel was chatting with her, I was busy communicating with Fatoumatta, who was on her way to Dakar with some girls also.

"Do you know we were going to spend a night here?" I asked her.

"Yes, I do! There's fear of something horrible happening in the Gambia. Just stay with my tactful Sable. She will safely bring you to me," she replied.

Sabel called my attention, and she took me to a robust old woman with a roguish smile. I think she was a retired teacher, a Gambian-Senegalese. We spent the night with her and left for Dakar very early in the morning on a single-decker bus. Honestly, I thought she was a belligerent type of person. I didn't have enough sleep; I was a bit worried about the distress Aunty Jestina and others might be going through searching for me in a giant city like Bo. On the bus, I asked myself many times if I was making a rod for my own back. Did I overreact? I couldn't get any answer from myself. I also didn't bother to ask Sabel about her relationship with the old woman because I didn't want to sound rude.

It was when we arrived in Dakar, about five minutes to the bus, she said, "You see that woman? She's a pensioner from France, also my late father's ex-wife. She's stingy more than miserly, which was why I bought some food from the food vendor before going to her house," Sabel explained.

"Probably she doesn't have money," I said.

"Says who? She has two duplexes in France, two townhouses in Dakar, and a block of flats in Banjul," Sabel said.

"Maybe she is trying to save for her children," I commented.

"Which children? She has only one child, and her daughter is wealthier than her. She hopes to take all her properties with her to the grave," Sabel said and beamed.

I checked the time when we arrived at the bus station in Dakar, seeing that it was 2:18 p.m. After a tedious gridlock on the way, we took a cab and went to an apartment building in downtown Dakar. As we were driving, I saw infrastructures I have never seen in my country—more beautiful than Freetown. At the apartment building, third floor, a black-skinned woman came out to welcome us. I thought she was Fatoumatta, but I realized by her tone and accent it wasn't her. She hugged us and introduced herself as Sainabou Secka. "Fatoumatta went out to the market to buy some food items," she said.

Sabel and Sainabou had a cordial relationship; I noticed it from the informal ways of addressing each other. Sainabou introduced me to two other ladies and two guys in a real Senegalese's skin.

The ladies were Alberta, Grace, and the guys were Sulay and Martin. Alberta was a Liberian, her parents migrated to the Gambia in the late 90s. Grace was a Nigerian, whose parents migrated to the

Gambia. Sulay was born to a Sierra Leonean father and Gambian mother, and Martin was from Guinea Bissau. But Martin's original name was Dacosta, and nicknamed himself after the late civil rights leader, Dr. Martin Luther King Jr., because of his great admiration for him.

Sainabou took us to the girls' room with three mattresses with a bedroom freezer. I never saw the apartment building and my roommates as a bellwether of change in my life, but I was more sanguine about my future. Fatoumatta went to the floor half an hour later after we arrived. I was in the girls' room battling with my thoughts, and I knew it was her from the tone of talking.

"Where's my darling, Martha?" she asked. I heard one of the guys telling her I was inside. I rushed out of the room and jumped on her. She pecked me on both cheeks before we sat down. I loved her barbed head with dyed, greyish hair, which she told me was her favourite colour.

After we had lunch, some took naps in the rooms and on the couch in the sitting room, but Fatoumatta and I sat on the veranda to chat.

"Are you okay?" she asked me many times during our discussion.

"Not sure I am," I replied to her.

"Well, maybe because you have never made such a tedious journey like that before; don't you think so?"

"Probably more than that. I'm still wondering whether I've made the right decision," I responded.

"Don't worry; you've made the right decision, my darling Martha. The good news is we are traveling to Europe next week," she said.

I looked at her and paused. I didn't ask her how, right away. "But I don't have a passport!" I told her.

"You don't need a passport, darling," she said to me.

"Why?" I asked

"Because you don't need it!" she emphasized.

The moment Fatoumatta made the statement, I knew exactly what she was talking about: crossing the Mediterranean Sea. I paused again, then went completely silent. She gazed at me attentively, waiting for me to ask her how, and indeed I asked. My instinct was right about it. Fatoumatta told me she had earmarked all her savings to make the journey, which is enough for me and her. I started shivering excessively. I lost myself, so I asked Fatoumatta to excuse me. I went to the bathroom and stayed there for a long time. I realized I had no choice but to agree with her. Until now, I'm still in bondage to my thoughts.

Sabel joined us in the veranda some minutes later with her usual gracious smile. I like Sabel; she was an earnest lady who told me there would be some challenges, but not tougher ones could stop us. "On the other hand, we have all earthly chance to make it through the sea, we can easily make the journey if only we are committed," Sabel said to me.

I became speechless again. I didn't realize Sabel knew about it. I tried to hide the hematoma near my elbow for Fatoumatta and Sabel not to see, but Sabel took notice of the swollen area on my hand and raised alarm. They immediately took me to a nearby pharmacy for medical attention. On our way back, Sabel left us and joined us with another girl, whose name was Awa. She looked quite haggard and was much quieter than me. I did have the chance to chat with her face to face the first time.

Awa was the only child to her deceased parents who were Gambians—a Wolof and Mandingo bred—was all she could tell me. It seems taboo for a potential migrant to express her pains to anyone except the white folks in Europe. I did what I could to dig her mind many times; she didn't say anything more than that. Fatoumatta and Sabel gathered us all in the sitting room to discuss the way forward on our journey to the white man's land. On that day, I got a clear view of how the journey was to start and end and all the money involved. We were to travel from Senegal to Mali, Mali to Algeria, and from Algeria to Libya. In Libya, we shall pay our way to onboard a boat through an agent. Nobody in our group made mentioned of the perils. They were saying it as if we were to move from one street to another street in paradise.

Fatoumatta, Sabel, and I went to the market the following morning, and when we returned, we were told Awa fainted and she had been taken to the nearest hospital. Before we got to the hospital, we were told Awa died even before they arrived.

I saw Awa's death as a stop sign. Her death signalled danger ahead, which I alone could see. I wanted to tell Fatoumatta to call off the journey right away; the desperation inside of her would have condemned me. Fatoumatta asked Sabel to take me home when she became aware of my nervousness at the mortuary. We passed by a bakery to collect loaves of bread for dinner from Sabel's new boyfriend. When we got home, I stood at the balcony for almost an hour, trying to think of a way out. *Was there a way out?* I asked myself.

Not too long after that, the others came home looking discouraged and disappointed. Fatoumatta came after them; she was so vigilant climbing the stairs. She called us all in the sitting room and gave us an update about the situation. Awa aborted a four-month pregnancy. She hadn't taken all the medication and the advice given by the abortionist.

Awa's family went for her body a couple of days later. Her guardians didn't even know she aborted a pregnancy, and that she ran away because of the humiliation from her family.

We were nine in the house; the sad demise of Awa brought us to eight. All the others were determined to cross the big sea, except me. My fears started to fade away whenever I thought about lanky Ansumana. With great courage and commitment, he made it to Europe the hard way. It means God will bless anything that he is committed to.

A few days after Awa's death, our apartment was a bit quiet, with no one-lines and jumping around like Grace and others usually do. Four days after Awa's family went for her body, Fatoumatta invited us in the sitting room, wanting to confer with us on the issue of Plan B. Sulay and Martin told us other migrants used the route from Mali, Niger to get to Libya, but none of us knew the route, even Fatoumatta, the master planner. Fatoumatta turned and asked me to give my take or whether I knew of any other option. I just smiled. I wanted to tell them to let our option B be abandoning the idea of coming, but I was afraid they would be offended by my comment. Throughout our stay together, I never heard anyone making a doubtful comment about reaching our destination. I didn't have the passion to listen to news directly due to the language. Sabel and Fatoumatta were our news channels.

Sulay was always acting like a fugitive. He would lock himself up in the room when we had a visitor, spoke in a low tone, and never made a call to check on family members. Martin, Grace, and I were like him. Sulay never left the building until the day we travelled to Mali; he would become aggressive if you asked him to take a walk around. Fatoumatta asked the others to stop getting him mad, so he won't feel he was the aggrieved person amongst us. Alberta seldom reached out to her mum through WhatsApp. One day, she put the phone on the loudspeaker and I heard her mum asking when she was leaving. So it means even her mother knew about her desire to come to Europe through Libya. Alberta's lost her father five years after they left Liberia, and her mother single-handedly took care of her. I couldn't tell how old Alberta was because her face looked ageless. Even though I had known Fatoumatta half a decade before I met Sabel, I became close to Sabel because of her more agile brain.

One thing I noticed was that all of them had money in dollars, and I had nothing—absolutely-zilch!

One morning, while Fatoumatta, Sabel, and I were going to the market, I asked them, "How am I going to do this, since I don't have money?" I felt agitated about what their replies would have been. Sabel gave me her gracious smile. Fatoumatta told me she had prepared financially for two of us. *Has she lured me into all this?* I asked myself. To my surprise, I saw the lunch lady's son at my formal school in Freetown. I hid behind Sabel until the boy and his friends passed me by unnoticed. Fatoumatta, who took notice of my action, didn't bother to ask me until we arrived home.

"Who were you hiding from," she asked me.

"Oh! One of the boys that passed by us at the marketplace," I replied.

"So you know them?" she asked me.

"I know the guy at the back!" I responded.

A day came when we finally fixed a date to start our journey. The delay was from Fatoumatta, who was contacting some people she left in the Gambia and those who had left the country because of the defiance of their president. Two days before our departure, Sulay became ill and too adamant to go to the closest pharmacy. He told us he would be okay, let's just leave as planned. Fatoumatta bought some medicine for him, assuming it was malaria. The eve before we departed, Sabel pleaded with him to go to the pharmacist. He still refused.

The day after our departure, in the evening, at around 3 p.m., all of us prayed in our different faiths, except Sulay, who was secretly shivering.

Fatoumatta said to Sulay, "Since you are too stubborn to go for medication, and still want to make the journey with us, you have the right to your life! Just remember, nobody and nothing will delay our journey," All of us smiled. Sabel hired a taxi and we drove to the bus station. We bought tickets and boarded the bus very quickly. There was no improvement in Sulay's health. It was just deteriorating every minute, and I was worried about him; so worried that I couldn't take my eyes off him. I kept asking him whether he was okay. He never answered no, and I never got tired of asking him.

Fatoumatta pinched me on my leg and whispered to my right ear, "You better stop asking him. If the people take notice of you, and anything negative happens, you would be asked to stay with him, and there I will leave you to perish with him. Do you understand?" I reluctantly nodded my head. Sabel looked at me and smiled. I didn't say a word to him again, but I was still observing him from a distance.

We left the bus station in Dakar at six o'clock prompt. Fatoumatta asked me to tell her about my father. I knew she wanted to get my attention off Sulay, who was in critical condition. I told her both parents have answered God's call.

"Thought you said you were living with your mother, who got married and travelled with your stepfather to the U.S.?" she asked me.

"She was a friend to the woman I knew to be my biological mother until she disclosed to us that she wasn't my mother. My parents died at a tender age," I replied to her.

"Why didn't you tell me all along?" she asked me. I didn't reply because I had no answer to her question. "It's okay, darling! I understand how painful it is," she said.

We got to one big junction, then the driver asked those who were interested to buy some food should do so. All seven of us got out of the bus with some passengers, except Sulay and some older women left on board. I heard Fatoumatta whispering to the others, so I went there to listen. "Good, you are here. Were you guys not there when I asked Sulay to see the pharmacist?" Fatoumatta asked us. We all nodded our heads.

"Were you guys not there when I told him sick folks don't make such a journey?" she asked us again.

We nodded our heads again.

"Whatever happens, I am expecting you all to pretend as if you do not know him, otherwise the driver will ask that person to stay with him at the hospital. Do you understand that?" she asked us. We nodded our heads again.

Some went to the latrine. Sabel, Fatoumatta and I bought some luscious fruits from the street vendors. We also used the latrine, and then we were on board the bus. Sulay was fast asleep. As we sat down, I whispered to Sabel, "Can I give Sulay one fruit?"

She answered, "No!"

Since I left Sierra Leone that very night, I started losing weight drastically. I ate, but not with pleasure. I smiled with pains in my heart; I walked lethargically; only those who knew me before could tell something was wrong. I pretended throughout my journey to this land I am in right now. My mood meant nothing to anyone. I became more pessimistic that all the horrible things I have heard about folks dying in the Mediterranean Sea, I was going to see it myself. It is obvious, water doesn't jump gutter. The darkness started to overcome the light as we go deep into the evening hours. I took out the note left behind by my father, which was the only expensive object I had with me. I tried to read the first few sentences to get myself motivated and hide it from the others, but smart Sabel asked, "Is that a letter from your boyfriend?"

I smiled and answered no.

"Then why are you hiding it from us? Such letters are sacred to people of your age," Sabel whispered.

"It may not be important to you," I commented.

"Says who? Everything is important to me. What note is that?" she asked.

"It's a note written by my father," I replied.

"Thought you said your father died before you were born, so how could he write it to you? Or the dead are now writing letters to the living."

"Well, he wrote it to me in advance before he died," I answered.

"Can I take a look at it?"

I reluctantly gave the note to her, and she read aloud.

"Hello Child,

Be you a girl or a boy, you are my child. Be you of any religion or gender, you are my child. I am your father, but I pray you don't face the problems that I faced in life. If you are a girl, you should be named after my mother, Miatta, and if you are a boy, you should be called Moses. Moses is not my father's name, because my father doesn't deserve to have a namesake. Please don't wonder why; some things are better left untold. If I tell you my story, you will never get over it, so I better leave you in harmony.

My name is Brima Peter Swarray, an ex-serviceman, also an amputee. I joined the army when I was seventeen years of age and was forced to retire at age fifty, because I and others may have been seen as worthless, or of no strength to defend our beloved country. I was retired, but my experience and knowledge in the military were not taken from me. After more than three decades of service to my country, all I received from my country was chicken feed. I am a son to the most wonderful woman in the world who died in pain. My father was the most foolish and irresponsible man in the world, never had respect for my mother and lacked regard for other women.

Now, what I am about to tell you is the main reason I wrote this letter. I must confess that I failed you, just like my father did. I should have been with you to watch you grow up as a patriotic citizen to planet Earth, to provide all your needs like God do for man, to protect and defend you as I did to my country, but if even I was alive, it wouldn't have been possible. I won't tell you not to serve your country, but serve her from the top, not the bottom. Those at the top make the decision, and those at the bottom are affected by it. I take responsibility if you fail or be successful.

I'm glad I served my country and my conscience diligently. I love you, sweetheart.

I love you.

Your dad.

Brima Peter Swarray."

As she was reading, I was crying. I never read the whole letter. I knew Sabel was gazing at me. She asked me to stop crying and be joyful.

As we were going, I desired to check on Sulay. He was looking so helpless. All my attention was focused on him. If I tried to make any moves, Fatoumatta and Sabel will be rankled with me. I didn't want Fatoumatta to start ranting at me as she did to Awa when she tried to discourage her from using the Algeria route. I didn't want to destroy the rapport between us. To get my attention from Sulay, I pretended to be sleeping, then I finally slept.

I woke again about an hour later, but I couldn't get my eyes off Sulay, looking at him with rapt care. I sensed from a distance that the lady who sat by him was frightened and uncomfortable. When night fell, and the driver turned off the light, I lost sight of Sulay. I tried again to move from my seat to check on him an hour after the light went off. "Where are you going?" Fatoumatta rasped. I sat back quietly. I thought she was sleeping. Sabel asked me to sit still. She told me Sulay may have caused havoc before traveling with us, but nobody knew the mess he might have caused. She continued saying things about Sulay—things I wasn't interested to hear until she started to ramble. "It seems all our advice has entered one ear and out the other. If you are identified with Sulay, I will deny you also," Sabel said to me and bowed her head. I sat still and thought about what Sabel told me. *This is another land. I know nobody, and I can't speak their language. If they desert me here, I will perish,* I said to myself.

Some time later, policemen stopped the bus driver. He was asked to park and wait, as some youths had gone on the rampage in the next village ahead of us, and we should wait until the situation calm down. We pull over by the roadside and waited for almost two hours. While we were there, Fatoumatta told me a story about her grandmother, who was gang-raped by some Guinean men on her way traveling from Freetown to Banjul around the late seventies. She got pregnant and gave birth to Fatoumatta's mother nine months after. Her grandmother kept the secret from her mother until she was forty years old, and Fatoumatta was fifteen. On her dying bed, she revealed the truth to Fatoumatta's mother about the incident that took place forty years before her birth. At the end of her grandmother's story, I was greatly confused and became pessimistic that something similar might happened to us. A man with dreadlocks, who sat next to Fatoumatta, smiled and asked, "What was the reaction of your mother when she heard the story?" We both paused because we never thought he understood the English language. We heard him speaking French and Wollof to the other women since on board the bus. "My mother became irked at my grandmother for hiding the truth from her for such a long time," Fatoumatta answered.

"My grandmother had a similar experience, and she never got over it until death," the man said. The man told us he's a contortionist, going to perform somewhere.

The engine started again, and we continued our journey. Ten minutes after, we arrived in a town called Koumpentoum, where we stopped again for passengers to buy food and use the latrine. When we went outside, Fatoumatta warned me again to stay away from Sulay, or I should be ready to face the consequences. Sainabou suggested that we should advise Sulay for the very last time to take another bus and return to Dakar immediately when we get another town called Tambacounda. There was a contradiction between those who agreed with Sainabou and those who disagreed with her suggestion. Martin, who was secretly dating Sainabou, disagreed with her. "We have done our best to stop him from making this journey, so whatever we do now will fall onto deaf ears," Martin said. Fatoumatta and Sabel nodded their heads to show support to Martin's comments. I stood out of the ring, listening thoughtfully to their conversation. I didn't say anything; my opinion wasn't needed. I nudged Fatoumatta's waist to let her know the Rastafarian was listening to us from a distance. Fatoumatta informed the group, and we all went separate ways without any agreement.

When we finally arrived at Tambacounda, we all gazed at each other, so was the Rastafarian. "Hope he didn't listen to all our conversation," Sabel whispered. Suddenly, we saw the Rastafarian man walk up an old woman and Sulay, have few words with them, and then returned to his seat. We noticed something fishy was going on, but no one amongst us had the guts to ask the man. We became worried about the unseen, but we became less worried when the Rastafarian man stepped off the bus when we arrived at Goudie. Once we got to Naye, the border town, the driver told us to stay inside the bus or find a location outside to sleep with other travellers we met there. We were to wait until the border opened at around six o'clock in the morning the next day. All seven of us went out, except Sulay, who sat helplessly. We slept in a parlour built for travellers. The next morning, Sulay was found dead on the bus.

Chapter 4

The driver was very worried; he called all the passengers together and told us, first in Wolof, later in Bambara. I turned to my right and asked Sabel to interpret what the driver had said. She put her right ring finger between her lips as a sign to be quiet. I turned to Fatoumatta to ask for interpretation, but she frowned and focused all her attention on the driver. My internal interpreter was telling me that the driver was asking about someone who knew Sulay. As I was listening to my instinct, I saw the old woman who sat behind Sulay quietly walk up and whisper to the driver. All eyes were on the old mama. The driver left our presence and returned with two police officers. Fatoumatta and Sabel were arrested and taken to the police station…I think for questioning. I tried to follow them to the police station, which was not too far, but Sainabou made a sign to me to stay.

With virulent criticism from the other passengers as they gazed at us, I knew my instinct was right. Everyone was so worried, except me, because I had no clue what was happening. About thirty minutes later, Sabel and the driver returned, our stuff was taken out of the bus, and they drove off. According to Sabel, they were censured by the police for keeping quiet when the driver was asking. It was the old woman who told the driver we had a cordial relationship with the deceased. "We told the police we warned Sulay not to come with us because he was sick, but he was stubborn," Sabel explained.

"So, what is the latest from the police?" Grace asked.

"The police said we should stay here until Sulay's family come for his corpse," Sabel replied.

"What? Do we know exactly when they are going to be here?" Martin asked.

"Have they contacted his family?" Alberta asked.

"Yes, the police have done that!" Sabel answered.

"How did they have his family's contact?" Sainabou asked.

"His pockets were searched, and the police found about nine hundred dollars and a list of contacts in a small diary," Sabel replied.

"What?" I exclaimed.

They all looked at me and smiled.

"His family is mad at him, and according to his uncle, Sulay stole one thousand five hundred dollars to make this journey, plus he was a gay." Sabel said

"And so?" Martin asked

"It isn't a secret among us that Sulay was a gay, and he was trying to run away from the marginalization in his community." Sabel continued. "You guys stay here; I must report back to the police!"

We moved and sat under a big tree. We didn't have breakfast until 1 p.m. A generous and virtuous man like Martin bought enough food for me alone. He knew I had no money with me; Fatoumatta was in the hands of the police. When the others went to buy food, Martin asked me whether I was financially prepared to make the journey. I just smiled.

"You know your success on this journey depends on Fatoumatta, don't you?" Martin asked.

I forcefully put a handful of food in my mouth to avoid answering him. He asked again how I met Fatoumatta, but I dodged his question again. It became visibly noticeable that I didn't want to answer him.

"I can't visualize what our lives would look like when we make it through the sea!" Martin commented immediately after the others returned. He was again ignored. "Haven't you guys imagined living out of Africa?" Martin asked.

"We imagine that every day! Is that not why we are making this journey?" Grace said.

All the questions they were asking weren't vital to me. All my attention was fixed on Sabel and Fatoumatta, who were not with us. I wondered what my life would have been like if they never came out of police custody. Even though I had some negative thoughts about my actions, I have never regretted running away from my auntie's house. The others were chatting next to me, but it sounded as if they were miles away from where I sat. I couldn't finish the food Martin bought me. As the youngest, the weakest, and the less experienced person in the group, I ran out of vitality and courage that very moment.

Fatoumatta and Sabel didn't show up until noon the following day. It was Sabel who went and delivered the message to us that Sulay's family had sent a representation to collect his body, and Fatoumatta and Sabel must go with the body to Dakar.

"What?" we all asked in chorus.

"Be patient, the journey is not over yet. We shall conquer the trials and tribulations of the devil. We shall be here tomorrow by His grace," Sabel said.

"Can I speak to Fatoumatta before you guys leave for Dakar?" I asked Sabel.

"No! If you try it, you would be taken in by the police for questioning," she answered.

She took out some money and gave it to me to cover my living expenses until they returned. "We shall overcome the prosecutions and problems." The ambiguous statement made by Sabel left me confused. I thought about what one female minister of God said when she was telling the story about Jonah in the Bible. When a group is trying to achieve something, and there's a Jonah among them, they'll never accomplish anything. I quietly bent down and slept under the tree.

We became the centre of attraction in Naye. People passed by every moment gazing at us. Sometimes we walked around to have minted ideas. One day, while we were walking around the border town, I heard two women speaking Krio. I looked at them for some time until they took notice of me. They knew I understood what they were talking about. One of them asked me in Krio, "Are you from Sierra Leone?"

"Yes, I am!" I answered.

We introduced ourselves in our main local dialect. They are both married to Malian husbands, and they have been there for over twenty-six years. Their names were Yealie and Kadie.

"What are you doing here?" Aunty Kadie asked me.

"I am traveling to Mali with my friends," I answered.

"To cross the sea?" she asked.

I paused and stared at them for some time. They told me hundreds of Sierra Leoneans had used the route to Libya, including Aunty Kadie's nephew, whom she had never met. Aunty Yealie warned us strictly about kidnappers on the road, and that not all cars lead to Libya. Her nephew was kidnapped, and his kidnappers demanded ransom. "My brother had to send money for his release. Don't think you are exceptional!" Aunty Yealie warned.

Once we returned to our original point, we met Fatoumatta and Sabel, who were patiently waiting for us. Their faces looked ashen as if they were sick. Their smell wasn't good, so they asked to take a bath. We had a brief meeting after they took a bath and again we disagreed. Sabel suggested we cross the border to Mali and spend another night there to get more information. Fatoumatta suggested we cross the border and board a bus to Bamako. Sainabou said we should cross over to Mali and get a bus that would take us directly to Agadez, the fifth largest city of Niger. Grace and Alberta said we should keep going; that time wasn't in our favour. I never gave my opinion because I didn't know where we were going and where we came from, so I avoided making any asinine suggestions. Sabel looked askance at Martin, expecting him to say something. Martin was a cool guy who doesn't talk much. Late Awa once called him an askew man, with no evidence.

We reached an agreement to cross the border to Mali first, then we saw what the others said. As we were trying to cross the border, Fatoumatta and Sabel were arrested again for failing to report to the police when they returned from Dakar. We spent more wasteful hours. They were released with a fifty-dollar bribe.

When we crossed over to Mali, we had another discussion on whether we should go straight to Bamako, Niamey, or Agadez. Martin, just like me, sat down quietly as if he wasn't part of the decision-making. Fatoumatta became mad at Martin's cold shoulder. Martin just smiled and told them he was in support of whatever decision they could come up with. I wondered what sort of a man can stand an asperity towards him. After thorough research, we noticed the buses traveling directly to Agadez were not in proper order, but passengers were comfortable with it. We met some youths who were making the same journey. Sabel suggested we observed their movement. Fatoumatta asked Sabel whether she wanted a change of plan. "Give me a few minutes," Sabel said as she walked towards one of the boys we suspected to be a migrant.

Sabel returned and asked me to go with her. While we were walking towards the people, Sabel told me they were from Sierra Leone. "They refused to talk with me. If you try to chat with them in your local language, they might listen to you," Sabel said.

I greeted them in Krio, and they responded in chorus. They were five in number, and the youngest one amongst them was of the same age as me. They called me their sister, and then I smiled. One of them stood behind, very observant, but refused to join our conversation. While we were chatting, the guy at the back looked at me for some time, walked behind possibly their leader, and whispered something to him.

The eldest amongst them asked me, "Are you from Bo Town?"

I was shocked. I answered yes.

"Your name is Miatta, right?" he asked me again. I became nervous and afraid to answer him.

"Don't be afraid! My friend here just whispered to me that your face is all over Bo Town as a missing person. Is that true?" the man asked me.

Sabel didn't understand what we were discussing, and when he saw the nervousness on my face, she asked me what the matter was. I didn't answer her either. "Martha?" she called.

The guy interrupted her and asked me, "Are you Miatta or Martha?"

I became confused. I looked at Sabel and the man, left and right. I replied to the man in Krio that my name is Miatta, not Martha. She couldn't pronounce Miatta, so they called me Martha.

"Martha, can you please tell me what's going on?" Sabel interrupted. I finally explained everything to Sabel. Since the man and his boys could understand the English grammar, they smiled.

Suddenly, Fatoumatta and the others joined us. "What's going on here, guys?" I again explained to them.

"Don't worry, many of us left home unbeknown to our families," Fatoumatta commented.

I told Fatoumatta and the others about the aspirations the men had to get to Libya and cross to Europe. Sainabou cast aspersions on the ambitions of the men and told us not to believe them. Fatoumatta wriggled her fingers, trying to figure out what to say, I think. I asked the men in Krio about the route they planned to use. According to their leader, they planned to travel from the border town straight to Agadez Region, Niger, then from there to Shabha, Libya, and from there to Tripoli (Libya), where they hoped to get an agent that would take them to the shore. We had been planning to travel from the border town to Bamako, Mali, then from there to

66

Gao, Mali, and from there to Agadez Region, Niger, then from there again to Adrar, Algeria, and from Adrar to Tripoli, Libya.

The men took out their map and showed us their route. We realized our plan entailed time and money. Disagreement arose again; some said we should abandon our plans and follow the route of the men, which was nice and economizing, while others said we should stick to our plans. Fatoumatta said she had heard the route from Agadez to Shabha is risky and unsafe for migrants; it will wreak destruction to our lives! If we pass through Agadez to Shabha, we will either be assailed by hunger and thirst or by local devilish Militias. Grace said going through Algeria involves money. "The money or your life—which one do you prefer?" Fatoumatta asked Grace, and then she kept quiet. There was a long pause. Sabel's face was wreathed with anger; Grace too. The men stood waiting to hear our final decision.

"Look here, my name is James. You guys shouldn't worry about the assailants—they are everywhere. Any path you choose to get to Libya, they will be there. We all just taking chances, but the dangers...no migrant can escape them," he said.

Fatoumatta still insisted we shouldn't get through Agadez to Shabha; instead, we should go directly to Bamako, and an agent there would lead us to Adrar, or get to Gao and leave for Adrar. She turned around to see our responses and realized she had not much support from the others. Our group became divided. Sabel said she would follow the guys from Sierra Leone. Alberta and Grace also agreed with her; thus, they left our group and joined the guys. Sainabou shifted, attempting to join Sabel. Despite all we went through, to see Sabel, Grace and Alberta going separate ways was more painful and sad. James gazed at us and smirked. Sabel hugged me and said, "Hopefully, we shall meet over the sea, or after death, if there is life after death." I almost cried as they turned their backs and walked away. My tears ran down my cheeks profusely.

Fatoumatta took us to a corner to revisit our plan, and with no objection, we agreed to go to Gao, Mali, and possibly get an agent there. It was a very tough decision to make; I could sense it from all of us. We couldn't believe the other guys left us so soon. The sorrow was all over our faces. Fatoumatta's eyes were blood red. We searched for transportation to Gao, and in the process, we met Sabel and the other guys, who were negotiating with a bus driver to reduce the fare for a woman and her daughter. I wanted to plead to Sabel to join us back, but it would sound as if I was driving a wedge between Fatoumatta and me, or between Sabel and Fatoumatta.

Sabel's farewell message gave me a sorrowful face to this day. Fatoumatta called Sainabou and Martin as they negotiated and bought four tickets. They came back to me a few minutes later, with preparedness on their faces. "We shall be leaving soon. The bus driver needs some more passengers to occupy the other seats," Sainabou said to me. We waited for hours, but they still couldn't get enough passengers to fill the bus. Subsequently, we were asked to spend the night at the bus station since it was already midnight. "Please, don't go too far; there are bad boys around!" the bus driver warned us.

Continually thinking about Sabel's farewell, I started developing paranoia. *Are we ever going to make it across the desert, or are we going to die there and vultures feed on our carcasses? Are we ever going to make it across the sea or drown and fish feed on our corpses?* I asked myself multiple times.

Whichever way death may come, I wasn't ready for it. I went to the latrine, and in the dark place, I cried bitterly for almost fifteen minutes.

Through vision I saw the servitude; through dreams I felt the slavery—the death ahead was vivid. Immediately, I went out of the stinking latrine and saw Martin waiting for me about five meters away from the door. I know he heard me crying. I wanted to ask him whether he was sent by Fatoumatta or if he did it voluntarily. They were worried about why I took so long in the lavatory. "She is safe," Martin said to the others. He moved away from Sainabou and Fatoumatta as we sat on an outdated settee about eight meters away, He asked me why I was crying. "Have you been forced to make this journey? Are you crying because Sabel and the others left us? I know your relationship with Sabel became very cordial before she left us; we are here with you, aren't we? See me as your elder brother and share your plights with me! Over my dead body would I let anyone hurt you?" Martin encouraged.

I didn't respond to any of his questions. The fact is, I couldn't express the way I was feeling, because it would have scared Martin too. I admired Martin's courage; he was so brave and believed in the leadership of a woman. In the end, Martin told me not to worry; we shall get to Europe soon and everything would be well.

When we returned to the others, we saw two other people sitting with them. Fatoumatta introduced them to us. They were Franck Drogba and Emmanuel Assemian from Ivory Coast; they were also trying to make the journey to Europe, desperately. They wore newly laundered clothes as if they had travelled by air. It seemed Fatoumatta, with her broken French, had explained everything to them and they were very willing to join our group. Emmanuel, whose grandparents migrated with his father to Ivory Coast from Ghana two weeks after President J.J Rawlings first took over, could understand English but not well. Emmanuel told us many things about his family the night they joined us. He expressed the hardship in their country in a sad tone. Franck was like Martin: he hardly talks. He would nod his head to whatever Emmanuel said. Emmanuel said they didn't want to lavish the money they made through hard labour; they were ready to invest on the journey.

I could still remember, on that very night, Sainabou told me beautiful stories about the Gambia—stories of courage and unique moral lessons. I listened to her word after word, and when she was finished, she asked me how hopeful I was. She didn't get any reply from me.

"When we finally get to Europe, my community will say they are proud of me. I became a laughingstock because I got pregnant and dropped out of school. So if I achieve this goal, I will have the laurels from my family—especially from my illiterate father," Sainabou said. "I know your parents would be worried about you," she continued.

Frankly, I was worried about the uncertainty, not those I left behind. In a very low-key tone, she sang melodious traditional Wolof songs to encourage herself. I noticed she was trying to cover up her fear, to hearten herself, so she sang until she fell asleep. I was probably the only one still awake, listening to my heartbeat—beating myself for the decision I had made—and fighting to have total control of my mind. The snoring of the others wouldn't let me sleep. I don't know how I fell asleep, but somehow I did. Then, suddenly, Fatoumatta tapped me on both my legs, and I woke up and checked the time. It was five in the morning; the cars were ready. She tapped the others and asked us to be prepared to continue our journey. Before we left our sitting position, Franck and Emmanuel came up with a very brilliant idea. They asked us to put our money in a place where it would be very difficult to find. They told us sometimes the drivers used to connive with government personnel, like the police or the military, to thoroughly search potential migrants and take away from them whatever valuables they could find. Franck, who could hardly speak, told us they got the information through some of their Ivorian friends who successfully manage to cross.

Fatoumatta took out eight hundred United States dollars, which I'm sure was the only sum left with her. She gave me four hundred to keep safely. I divided the money: two hundred in my pants, and two hundred in my pocket bible. I watched Fatoumatta put some of her money in her unkempt hair, and the rest in a position I can't remember.

We boarded the bus at around 6 a.m. and waited until 7 a.m. before we left. All those times, I wondered when I would breathe freely again; when would I wake up with the sun and smile like an innocent child. I sat next to Martin, listening to his interesting things about Guinea Bissau. He was born and raised in Banjul, but he travelled to Bissau at the end of every academic year. His happy mood changed suddenly after we crossed two checkpoints. He sounded suspicious about the unseen, asking God to come down and help carry his fears.

"Are you okay, Martin?" I asked him.

"Yes Martha, I am okay," he responded, as he turned his face to the window. "There are risks on the way. You know that, right?" he continued. I couldn't see his face. "Because of our identities we are putting our precious lives on the line." Nervously, he dipped his right hand in his pocket and took out a pen and a diary. With his shivering hand, he wrote his family contact numbers and address on two pieces of paper, then he gave the one piece of paper to me. "Keep this paper for me, in case something goes wrong. Please contact my family and let them know how much I love them and how much I was ready to make sacrifices for them. You may do the same, should you like to!"

I rejected the paper at first, though later I felt the same way, but giving out my family contact was still scary. I didn't want any of my family members to know my whereabouts.

For the first few checkpoints we passed, I saw the driver handing something over to police, soldiers, and other government officials like I saw while traveling from Sierra Leone to the Gambia, through Guinea. The situation started changing as we gradually approached Gao. After five checkpoints, as I was counting, passengers were asked to step out of the bus for security reasons, and government officials were becoming very hostile to some passengers from Anglophone countries. At other checkpoints, they would be aggressive to their fellow nationals.

When we got to the last checkpoint in Gao, we were asked to step out of the bus, a beautiful policewoman demanded our identity cards. All my friends presented identity cards except me. The policewoman, fluent in both English and French, asked me, "Why are you not with an identity card?" I bowed my head as fear ran down my veins.

"How old are you?" the policewoman asked

"I'm fourteen years," I replied.

"Where are you from?" she asked me.

"I'm from Sierra Leone," I answered.

"And where are you going?" she asked me again. I became very nervous, and the woman noticed it from my body and voice. She told me not to be afraid; she won't hurt me. "Come with me!" she ordered me, while the driver and the other passengers were patiently waiting. She took me to a very tiny building. Inside was an office with few other police officers.

"You see, these officers in this building don't understand English. I'm a mother to three girls and one boy, but I'm a devil to dishonest people and a good angel to the righteous. If you tell me the truth about your destination, I may let you go. If you lie, I will lock you up for days and send you back to your country. Where are you going?" she asked me. I wasn't convinced at all, but I had to tell her the truth because I had no choice. "So you're going to Libya, right?" she asked.

I slowly nodded my head to answer.

"Letting you go now; I'm paving a way for you to die in the sea. If I return you, I would be seen as a bad person to you, right?" she asked.

I had nothing absolutely to say, so I kept quiet.

"You may go. Take responsibility for your decision!" she ordered me.

When I went out, I heard the driver and other passengers grumbling. Fatoumatta hugged and kissed me, then we boarded the bus and it drove off. Some passengers became moody; they remained grumpy until we arrived at the bus station in Gao. Franck and I waited until all the other passengers went down before we walked majestically out of the bus. As I watched through the windows, I became frightened. The men dressed exactly like our Imams in Sierra Leone, the women like their wives, purely in Islamic outfits. I heard Sainabou shouting my name. "Martha? Martha? Hurry up!" I waited, because I wanted to have a few minutes to observe the area very well, but I'm not sure that was the same reason Franck did. He told me we can't control what was to happen. I didn't know him to be a fatalist. It was obvious: the destiny of our journey was unknown.

Fatoumatta and the others asked Franck and me to wait next to the bus while they searched for an agent. We had the intelligence from Sabel's schoolmate, who successfully made it to Italy. Migrants should get an agent to get them through the Algeria border. I felt my waist throbbing after long traveling, and my eyes paining. From a distance, I noticed a man in his late fifties looking at us, and he did for long in a fatherly way. He smiled and waved to me. Franck nudged me and pointed his hand towards Emmanuel and the others. "Stay focused!" he said. That was the very first time I heard him speaking English with boldness. There was no one among us with a big bag like a backpack or suitcase, except Sainabou with her rucksack. We were all with small bags like a shoulder bag, which Fatoumatta bought at the bus station in Dakar to put a few pants in, and I was with a handbag bought by Sabel.

I couldn't pull my attention from the old man. I slowly turned to look at him, but he was already by my side. "Hello, my children, do you need help?" the man asked.

"No, sir!" I replied to him.

"Okay my children. I will be around in case you need any assistance!" the man said and strolled away.

We stood in the same place for over fifty-five minutes, waiting to see an end to the negotiation between our guys and the agent, and it was a nail-biting hour of standing. The old man came to us again and said to me, "You guys come and have a seat!" I looked at Franck to see his response, but he made no moves. I knew he didn't understand what the man said to us. I elbowed him and made a sign that we should follow the man. He was reluctant at first but later followed me.

A few minutes later, Fatoumatta came over and whispered in my ear. She needed about one hundred dollars to reach an agreement with the agent and to change the other hundred to their local currency. The old man and two of his friends were watching us, so I asked for the latrine to find a convenient place to remove the note. Walking towards the latrine, at the corner, I took out the money from my hair and gave it to Fatoumatta. Once we got back to the same position, I saw Albert, one of the Sierra Leoneans we met at the Senegal border, with Mali. Anxiously, he was also looking for an agent, but I was more concerned about why he deserted his group and moved on his own and the whereabouts of Sabel and the others. He told us they had travelled to Bamako, the capital city of Mali, then from there to Benena (also Mali), then from there to Agadez (Niger), then from Agadez to Libya.

"It's just a waste of money," Fatoumatta said as she ambled away from us.

After Fatoumatta left, I asked Albert why he didn't join them.

"It's complicated, my sister!" he replied.

"Have you got an agent to Tamanrasset?" Albert asked me.

"The others are on it!" I answered him. He left us and joined them.

Franck stood gazing at a very old beggar and his son, or grandson, begging under the hot burning sun. He gabbled first, I had to ask him to repeat what he said; he gave me a bland smile. Emmanuel once said Franck is a person who blabbered a lot, and I thought he was on it. I focus my eyes on Fatoumatta and the others, but at the same time hearken to his voice. He was saying, "Oh vie! Oh, vie! Vie est dur!" I tried not to look at his eyes until the others joined us. Fatoumatta took notice of Franck's sad mood and the tears running down his cheeks.

"Why is Franck crying?" Fatoumatta asked me.

"He was staring at the old beggar, and I later heard him blabbering," I replied.

"Blabbering about what?" Sainabou interrupted.

Emmanuel smiled and said, "Don't worry, Franck has a humanitarian heart, so he sheds tears easily when he sees things like that. It's one of the reasons he embarked on this journey: he wants to go to Europe, hoping to make money and help the poor."

We all sympathized with him. I became more sympathetic, knowing he was an orphan and his only sister died months back. I understood he was trying to blank out his trying experience.

Fatoumatta took out the bread from her tiny bag, cut it into bite-sized pieces, and shared it with us, but Franck rejected his shares. The bizarre situation we found ourselves in; pitiful things never bothered us. Fatoumatta told me we should be ready, as the agent had gone to the driver to do the payment.

"Is the remaining money in a safe place?" she asked me in a low tone.

"Yes, it is," I answered.

"Keep it safe; it's the only money we have left," she warned.

Not too long after, the agent came back, took out some cards, and gave them to Fatoumatta. He told her he was sorry; the cards were not enough.

After he left, I asked Fatoumatta, "Why didn't he give you the complete tickets?"

She told me the cards were not tickets to the bus; they were passes we should use at any checkpoints and at the Mali border with Algeria. "It will lessen the expected humiliation," she commented.

We were on board the bus not too long before some other potential migrants from the Gambia and Senegal arrived at the bus station in Gao. They were blessed with excellent smiles and were so excited to have finally been in Gao, except for one with bleary eyes. As migrants, we were intimate, so we started up a conversation. Only two, out of the three boys from the Gambia could fluently speak English, the one can only speak one of their local dialects. They were Ebrima, Mousa, and Modou.

"Is Modou a true Gambian?" I whispered into Fatoumatta's ear.

"Yes, he is. Why did you ask?" Fatoumatta replied.

"Is English not the official language in the Gambia?" I asked.

"Yes, it is. Why?"

"I wonder why Modou can't understand a single word in English."

Fatoumatta laughed and said, "We've people like him in all Anglophone countries. They don't value the English language, but they want money from England. We have a certain tribe in the Gambia; they are after money, not education. Modou is from that tribe."

Fatoumatta was related to one of them. Ebrima's stepmother was Fatoumatta's aunt; Ebrima's eldest sister was a wife to Fatoumatta's late stepbrother. Sainabou also came from a blended family. Her father had three children before he divorced Sainabou's mother and married her rich stepmother with four grown-up children.

We were distracted by a bleating lamb tied at the front of the bus. The driver with a bushy beard boarded the bus and counted us. "It's time to go," Fatoumatta whispered. I slowly bowed my head and prayed to God Almighty for over ten minutes. It was no secret I was afraid, but I had no choice but to face the unseen. It seemed like forty percent of the passengers were possible migrants. It was so simple to notice the desperation on our faces, though some were calm. I never knew we were embarking on a three-day journey from Gao to Tamanrasset. I had little or no idea about the challenges ahead of us. Some migrants said it was unstable; some said otherwise when you have money and cooperate with the securities on the road. But desperate migrants didn't care about the hazards.

On board the bus, we had migrants from Sierra Leone, Guinea Conakry, Senegal, Liberia, Burkina Faso, Mali, Ivory Coast, Ghana, and even a Togolese, who was stabbed to death together with Martin on our way to the Algerian border. Ebrima and his colleagues were left behind.

Something suddenly happened before we even left the park. Ebrima and Modou decided not to go with us. They jumped out of the vehicle and went to see their agent; we never saw them again. The driver had to wait again to fill their spaces.

The driver said something before he started the engine of the minibus. Some of the passengers, especially the Malians, hooted with laughter. I looked at Fatoumatta and forced myself to smile. No one in my group understood what the driver said, but the Malian-Senegalese guy behind us interpreted the driver's statement to us. What he said wasn't even funny. How could he tell his passengers to get ready to cry? The guy told us sometimes women and girls—even some boys—cry when they are faced with tough humiliations on the road. I anticipated it, and my hope was worse than what he said, but the driver's horrendous statement didn't deserve my amusement. What amused me was a man who claimed to be a Malian lecturer on sabbatical, who was traveling to Tamanrasset to broaden his horizon. I was not convinced at all. How could a well-educated man choose an unsafe zone as a vacation site? And it was his fifth time.

Once we got to the first checkpoint, we were asked to step out of the bus to make a queue. One by one, we were required to make five thousand CFA. Three of the passengers, including the self-claimed lecturer, couldn't pay the money, but the officers pretended not to be aware of him. They focused their attention on the two other passengers. The officers commanded the driver to drive off and leave the two other passengers who had refused to make the payment. The majority of the passengers on board the bus were angry, but then again we had no voice in such a hornets' nest. He drove about fifty meters away from the checkpoint, and then he stopped and waited for the two passengers as they hopped into the bus. With tears in their eyes, they told us the officers hit their legs with the rode on their hands.

The bus was the opposite of a cheetah—very slow, very uncomfortable! While wondering why the said lecturer didn't pay, Fatoumatta interrupted my thoughts. "Are you following what is going on?" she whispered.

"No!" I replied.

"Be attentive! Did you know Mr. Lecturer didn't pay a penny?"

"Yap!" I answered.

"Set an eye on him from a distance!" Fatoumatta said.

What was so scary about him? He paid attention to everything passengers were discussing on the bus. He took out a small piece of paper and wrote down something. I also knew he was fluent in French, some Malian and Senegalese local dialects, and probably English, because of the book I saw lying on his lap, which was titled *The Reversal of Roles*. He turned sharply to the Gambian guy who was telling his friend to put his one hundred dollars under the pad of his trainer. Two other boys did the same and the man gazed at them also. He alone would cackle with pleasure to every repugnant gag made by the driver.

I felt sleepy, but couldn't sleep because of the task given to me, and a very high temperature of over 40 degrees centigrade. I admired some of the passengers who were able to sleep comfortably— sweating, snoring, and snorting. It wasn't long before Fatoumatta and Sainabou also fell asleep.

We arrived at another checkpoint with bivvies' on both sides of the road. The driver pulled over and asked us to step out respectfully. Fatoumatta, who was desperate to know the reception that would be given to the lecturer, stood behind him in the queue as we walked up to the officers. I ambled behind Fatoumatta. When it was his turn to cooperate with the officers, he took off his Panama hat and smiled at them, then strolled away. Fatoumatta nudged me. Four passengers, including the previous two, couldn't pay the usual sum to the officers, so the driver was asked to leave them there. Two Good Samaritans from the Malian group made the payment for them. I heard them saying "Merci, merci!" But the lecturer said "Merci bien" to the Good Samaritans. The driver looked through the rear-view mirror and smiled at the lecturer. Fatoumatta elbowed me again to pay attention.

Fatoumatta, who sat at my right, told me some of her plans when she arrived Europe. She never loved to stay in Italy, telling me the land has flown with thousands of migrants, so for refugees to start a new life would be a bit tough. A friend of hers who managed to get to Germany from Italy advised her to do the same with the given guidelines. She learned some basic words in the German language to help her on the journey. She did a lot of research about Europe, just like Fatoumatta and Sabel. Sainabou's final destination was France to learn French and have the opportunity to speak two international languages. I had no final destination; in fact, I had never planned to make such a journey in my life. Fatoumatta lost focus on the lecturer when he finally fell asleep.

He suddenly awoke when we got to another checkpoint, and this time, the men on the road didn't look like government officials. They were a gang of robbers or militias. They violently hit the bus with their bare hands and shouted at the driver to pull over in Bambara. We all became panicky, except the lecturer, who was pleased. He was the first to scoop out of the bus even before the bus driver. We saw him thawed with the militias as if they had known each other before. He gave them the piece of paper he was writing on. I started reading the twenty-third Psalm in my heart. The gang was very harsh and aggressive to us with no beam on any of their faces. They brutally dragged the two Gambians out of the bus and took off their sneakers. They searched the sneakers and took out the dollars under the pads of their trainers. The situation became tenser when their leader took out a dagger and stabbed Martin and one of the Togolese men to death when they delayed to obey their commands. Sainabou and two other ladies fainted instantly. I watched Martin, a very calm and humble guy, bleeding to death right in front of us. He stretched his right hand towards me and took his last breath. Their leader asked us to hand over all our money and valuable stuff to his boys, or he would slaughter us all. Passengers were shivering as they took out the money from all part of their bodies and handed it over. I saw them pull Martin's dead body to the back of a tent. Then they came back and did the same to the body of the Togolese man. I attempted to duck my left hand into my pants to give them the dollars, but Fatoumatta held onto my hand very firmly.

I couldn't stand the tears as they ran down my cheeks. The leader stood in front of me and pointed the dagger at my forehead. My soul drooped when I smell Martin's blood on it. I thought I heard his blood crying. He gently pushed the dagger to my forehead and giggled. "Your brother! Your brother, huh?" he asked me. Martin's blood from the dagger dropped down Boom! Boom! Boom! The drops splitting the ground like earthquake. The militia's leader punched me hard in the face, and then I fainted.

Chapter 5

I regained my consciousness a few hours later when we were not far from the next town. Fatoumatta and Sainabou sat on my right side, shedding tears, and Emmanuel was busy fanning me. Franck was reading his Bible, and some passengers were bitterly crying, while others were grumbling. The driver was consoling us. I wiped the gore from my legs, which I thought came directly from my body. I drank some water. I felt like returning home but articulating my feelings to my friends was a problem for me. Nobody talked to me about what happened after I lost consciousness until midnight. I gently sat, looking at the setting sun as I reminisced about our pains and agony. I heard Fatoumatta and Sainabou murmuring about what happened and how the bus driver may have conspired with the criminals to extract money from us.

Eventually, we came to another checkpoint. From a distance, we knew they were government officers in uniforms. At sun set hour, I felt a bit of relief.

As usual, we were asked to get off the bus. The driver explained to the officers what happened, in Bambara, I think. They took a lengthy statement from him, while we waited in a sun-drenched area. I thought the officers would not ask us for anything, due to what had happened to us, but instead asked us to make a queue and collected the usual sum from us. That was the moment I thought about Martin and the Togolese guy and I burst into tears!

A beautiful policewoman, with sunburned skin, approached me. She took out a handkerchief from her pocket and wiped my face, "It's okay now, my daughter," she said to me. I was surprised to hear her speak the English language in such a remote Francophone country. She shook my hand and secretly passed a small card to me. All the passengers stared at us as the woman hugged me tightly, but never had they taken notice of the paper she passed me.

I squeezed the paper as we boarded the bus again. Her emollient smiling got me a bit soother. I opened my palm and showed the paper to Fatoumatta and Sainabou. It looked like a complimentary card, but it wasn't. It contained her name boldly typed and her signature on the back. We knew nothing about the use of the card at that present moment, and we were also scared to show it to anyone. "It could be a pass, in case of any harassment on the way," Sainabou said.

"Maybe!" Fatoumatta said.

The wasteland was extremely dark; the only light was from the headlight and the taillight of the broken bus. I didn't slumber or rest, nor did Fatoumatta, Sainabou, Franck and Emmanuel. Our eyes were open, waiting to see what would happen. I could remember Sainabou encouraging Franck to stay awake when he felt sleepy. We had the feeling we were heading for danger, but we tried not to say it. Fatoumatta crossed her hand around my shoulders as she cradled me, reassuring me not to feel discouraged. "We shall overcome these challenges and get to Europe by the Grace of Allah. We shouldn't expect much from an emergent nation like this," she said.

Suddenly, there was an argument between the bus driver and a woman in her late forties, who lost probably everything to the criminals. The argument was in Bambara, but the Malian guy behind us interpreted what they were saying to each other. The woman boldly accused the driver of conniving with the criminals, or may have gotten knowledge about their presence there, but underestimated their intelligence. The driver emphatically denied the accusations and threatened to drag the woman out of his bus; let her perish in the wilderness. His statement made the other Malian passengers mad, including our interpreter. The bus became very noisy and uncomfortable for us until after almost thirty minutes when we finally had peace. I could remember the man who approached us and offered us a comfortable place to sit down at the car park. I could remember him telling us that there was no bus to Tamanrasset, only open trucks. But there was none at that moment." Was he trying to tell us we are embarking on the wrong vehicle?"

We arrived in a very big town at around two in the morning, where the driver asked us to rest for a couple of hours.

The name of the town is Kidal. Yes, that was what I heard when we were leaving in the morning. We had wanted to stay on board the bus until we departed from the town, but the driver strictly told us he will lock the bus and sleep in one of the houses in the town, so if we stay on the bus, we shall have to stay there until he returned. We unwillingly stepped out of the bus and joined the other passengers under a very big tent next to a police station. Next to our Malian interpreter, I sat still—no sleeping, no nodding. I thought about all the horrible things we had gone through since we started our journey to the new world. I thought about Awa, who died at the Senegal border with Mali. I thought about Sabel, Alberta, and Grace, who left our group and joined the others. I doubted we were going to meet again. I thought about calming Martin, who was stabbed to death with the Togolese guy under the hot burning sun. Tears ran down my cheeks once again but I didn't snort or wheeze. I fought so hard for homesickness not to overcome me. Fatoumatta prepared a place for me to lay my head and rest, but I refused. I didn't refuse because of the discomfort of the place, but because I was worried bad people might come and kill us all or feared not waking up. Oh well; I had that thought throughout our precious time in that desert.

There was a guy in a local outfit that started leering at me since we boarded the bus in Gao. At night, I saw him roaming up and down as if he was searching for something. Our Malian interpreter told me the man was frustrated because of the calamity some militia brought on him.

"How?" I asked him.

"Well, they sacked him, and a few days later militias killed his wife and his daughters," he answered. "But he doesn't attack people."

I felt pity for him, but how did he get to know the man? "How do you know him?" I asked the interpreter.

"He was my next-door neighbour," he replied.

The driver returned to us after three hours thirty minutes and asked us to board the bus, and lethargically we did. A flat-chested Malian-Ghanaian woman collected a piece of paper from the ground and gave it to me. It was the paper given to me by the Malian female police officer at the previous checkpoint. "Merci!" I thanked her and smiled. I wondered how she knew the paper belonged to me. During the nap, I noticed the majority of us on the bus were trying to flee our countries because of different reasons. The depression from our various homes and the tough challenges on the journey gave us all bitter faces.

Even though fear is a fact of life, I feared about the future. I feared the danger; the unexplainable pains were there, and they brought fear to my mind. I feared the unknown and the unseen. I fear death, which I never wanted, but expected to come. All the fear I had started to fade when I became so determined to reach Europe. Emmanuel and I took out our Bibles, Franck was with his missal, and Fatoumatta and the majority of the other passengers were reading the Quran. About an hour and a half, after we left the previous checkpoint, one woman fainted. The aisles on the bus were too small for passengers to leave their seats in a rush. They struggled to bring her back to normal. There was no medical practitioner on board the bus, so passengers were just guessing what to do and trying to help. Emmanuel squeezed through the aisle and rushed to the front seats where the woman was lying motionless with saliva coming out of her mouth. He called for water to be poured on the woman's head, albeit, he had no experience. I took out a bottle of water, but it was hot because of the heat. Emmanuel told me it didn't matter.

Could it be because of fear? Do people collapse because of fear?

I asked myself. A woman sitting on the second roll in front of us said, "Yio wa dara, Owọn mi."

I quickly turned and look at her. "What did you say?" I asked her with curiosity.

"I said she will be okay," the woman answered. "You look pretty much like a Yoruba woman!" she continued.

"Are you from Nigeria?" I asked her again.

"No, my daughter. I'm from Benin."

"Are there Yoruba's in Benin?"

"Yorubas are everywhere," she smiled.

I stood at the side of the Yoruba woman as I watched Emmanuel apply all his inexperienced skills to bring back the woman to normalcy. After about half an hour, he finally gave up on her and laid her straight on the floor.

"Is she going to be okay?" I asked Emmanuel.

"I hope so!" he replied.

I staggered back to my seat and sat calmly. Almost all the passengers were worried about the outcome of the situation. Suddenly, a short woman stood up. She took a leaf out of a tiny bag tied around her waist and chewed it in front of us, then spit it on the collapsed woman's face.

"She's a traditional healer?" I whispered to Fatoumatta, who focused on what the woman was doing.

"Ssshhh!" She turned to me and put her finger between her lips. There was an ominous silence on the bus. I closed my eyes and started praying in my heart, calling on the omnipotent God. What I was saying in my heart jumped to my lips, and abruptly Fatoumatta nudged me. "Is she okay?" I asked her.

"No! You are taking people's attention with your lousy prayers!" she answered.

The traditional healer asked the young girl, who was with the woman, whether the woman lying was her mother.

"Yes, she's my mother!" the girl replied. The girl stood and lolled by her seat as she stared at the woman. In my mind, I kept telling myself that the woman was an alone mother.

The traditional healer walked wearily back to her seat as if she had given up on the woman. She asked the driver to drop the woman at the next checkpoint, saying she would die if she continued the journey. We were all concerned about why the woman and her daughter should be dropped. Suddenly, the driver pulled up and asked the traditional healer, "Why? Why?"

"This woman has had a male spirit since she was a girl, and this spirit doesn't want her to get married or leave Mali. That's why all the men who wanted to marry her would die eventually. The spirit had warned her not to make this journey, but she's very stubborn to the spirit this time, so now it has taken her soul away until her body is returned to Gao," the traditional healer said.

All of us, including the driver, became nervous when the woman said the male spirit had been following us since we started our journey at Gao. One of the passengers asked the driver how far the next checkpoint was.

"It will take an hour at the longest!" the driver answered.

Eighty percent of the passengers agreed to leave the woman at the next town/checkpoint to save her life, except the driver who disagreed, as some passengers suspected him of dating the woman. "Do you want me to leave her on this long-haul route?" the driver asked.

"Yes, if you want her to survive!" the traditional healer replied.

The driver angrily started the bus engine and sped up. I sensed the disappointment and nervousness in the faces of some of the other passengers. About two minutes before we got to the next town, the woman regained her consciousness. We were all surprised. She took her seat and acted as if nothing had happened to her. When we reached the long-awaited town, the woman majestically walked out of the bus, leaving her daughter behind without saying a word to anyone—not even the driver. She didn't join the queue to be searched and be questioned by the officers, but her daughter did. She conked the girl and removed her from the queue violently. We had two things that distracted our attention: one was two Senegalese dragged out of the queue by a Malian soldier, and the other was a conjuror, who was conjuring a distance away from us. I had to focus my attention on the one that was more important at that very moment, which was the Malian soldiers and the two Senegalese migrants. Our interpreter told us the two Senegalese migrants refused or probably didn't have money to pay the officers. The soldiers took them under a tent and asked them to stand.

One of the Senegalese paid before the officer was done attending to us. Malian Good Samaritan honoured the bill of the other Senegalese. It was around midday, and our interpreter and some other passengers started grumbling at the driver for refusing to give us time to buy some food. The more passengers that grumbled, the more he pressed his foot down. He said we wanted to waste his time, and that time was against him, and if any passenger refused to pay at any checkpoint, he wouldn't be bothered to wait on him or her. Most passengers got edgy any time the driver raised his cracked voice to address a certain issue.

Finally, passengers became calm again. Our interpreter told us a story about his nephew...how he safely made it to Germany from

Mali. "Even he himself faced tough challenges moving from Mali to Libya. The sea was very calm the night he boarded the boat, as if Allah was standing on the water that very moment," he said. "OH! I pray Allah would stand on the water for us the day we embark the boat. If not, I will die, because I swim like a rock!"

"So getting to Eden, one must die to arrive," I mumbled to myself.

Fatoumatta turned towards me and said, "Please, do not say your worthless prayers here! Why won't you learn to pray in your heart?"

I acted as if my attention was focused on Franck and Emmanuel, who were chatting, to avoid answering her irritating question.

The driver unwillingly stopped and asked passengers to buy food at the edge of the town. Despite the fact that there were almost half of the passengers who grumbled at the driver, only a few Malian passengers went out to buy food. While I was dithering on what to do, Sainabou elbowed me and asked whether I was okay. She wanted me to focus on Franck and a Malian girl, who were looking at each other with distrust. "Franck, are you okay?" I asked. I got his attention. He didn't reply but dove into his coat and took out his pocket Bible.

"Do you think Franck and that Malian girl are at logger heads?" I asked Sainabou.

"I don't know!" she responded.

"An introvert like Franck doesn't deserve such expression on his face!" I commented.

Sainabou just hissed at me and put on a stony face. I thought she was seriously mad at me because of the kindly comment I made about Franck, until later when she started expressing to me how much she would miss her child. She told me some Gambian folks who had made it to Europe advised her to take her child along. "Don't you think my child would perish under such humiliation and dehumanization we were undergoing?" she asked me and forced herself to smile. I sensed the pains in her smile; I saw the agony that most young African mothers go through. "I don't want to have my child grow up just like me. My child is the reason I am embarking on this uncertain journey," she continued.

A man came by, dressed in a military uniform with a pistol around his waist, where the bus was parked. His face looked very disgruntled and depressed, which got most of us cowed. Immediately, he entered the bus and counted us, then stepped out to meet the driver. He chatted with the driver in a whispering tone before he left. And the passenger he was complementing to Franck was the soldier's daughter, who was going to Tamanrasset to visit her grandparent.

"She's beautiful!" Sainabou whispered to Emmanuel.

"Thank you, guys!" the girl commented.

We were all surprised. "So you can speak English?" Fatoumatta asked her.

"Fluently!" she answered.

"Where did you learn it?" Sainabou asked her.

"In Ghana!" she replied.

"Are you a Ghanaian?" Fatoumatta asked her again.

"A Malian-Ghanaian. My father, the military man who ushered us in, is a Malian. And my mother is a Ghanaian," she responded.

Her name was Bintou Toure. She told us her father and mother met in Accra, where they got married and moved with her mother to Mali. I relaxed in my seat as I thoughtfully listened to her as she responded to every question. I craned over the seat in front of me to see the other new passengers. As soon as I took my sitting posture, we heard a gunshot from the checkpoint ahead of us. We all cowered behind the seats—the very first time to hear a gunshot in flesh. The driver wasn't even panicky. He laughed at us as he drove towards the checkpoint.

"Come down!" he shouted at us.

Our new friend Bintou Toure emanated confidence, as she was the first passenger to step out of the bus. Her relatives followed before the rest of us were confident enough to walk out. As I watched through the window, I saw Bintou being hugged by one of the officers at the checkpoint, before her relatives and she crossed over. The officers at that checkpoint were very kind as they allowed two passengers to go even though they couldn't afford to pay the pass fee. When we boarded the bus again, I had the opportunity to personally converse with Bintou, and she was very responsive to all my questions. She told me she was very fortunate to go to school, because her father wanted her to, and there were a lot of girls of her age who were waiting for men to woo them. She said as one of the few lucky girls in her community to attend Western school—and having the opportunity to speak English, French, and little local dialect—made her more popular and regarded by women and girls in her community, especially her age mates. She took out a portrait of herself in her school uniform and showed me and the others.

"I started a voluntary campaign to encourage children to go to Western school and encourage parents to send their children to gain a better education. My family name almost became mud in gutter, so my dad asked me to back off. I haven't given up the idea to emulate great African women—to make a positive change in my community. The time will come again soon, very soon!" Bintou said.

I was speechless. She was so bold and brave. She didn't bother to ask where we were going; she just wished us a successful journey and egged us on as she stepped out of the bus a few hours later.

Fatoumatta nudged me and whispered in my ear, "She knows about our destination, doesn't she?"

"It seems so!" I answered her.

"Did you reveal our plans with her?" Fatoumatta asked again.

"No! Why should I?"I asked her.

Bintou waved to us as we drove off.

"They are nice people, aren't they?" I asked Fatoumatta.

"I don't know, darling! You made a great fuss of them; they are just like any other Malian. Haven't you felt all that the Malians had done to us?" Fatoumatta replied.

I noticed Fatoumatta was mad—not at me, but at Sainabou, whom she earlier thought was a backseat driver. Through my observation, I realized when Fatoumatta is angry, everyone around her would shower her madness, so her behaviour never baffles me. I didn't bother to ask; I just sat down quietly.

As I sat calmly, I thought about Martin and the things he told me about his family. Would I be able to contact them? If I do, where am I going to tell them they buried his body? They will see me as a bad person if I can't answer their barrage of questions! But again, it will be really bad if they don't know whether their son is alive or dead. Somehow, many migrants have died trying to cross the Mediterranean Sea unknowingly to their families. Should I let Martin be counted as one of them? I tried not to show any sign of fear in our case. Sunday sent me a short message, reassuring me everything was going to be okay.

When I woke up after a nap, I noticed Fatoumatta or Sainabou may have put a piece of cloth on my head to save me from the heat.

"Did you dream about your ancestors?" Fatoumatta asked me. I just checked my watch. She knew I was hurt, so she said funny things that she thought would make me smile.

As the sun was setting on our second-day journey to Tamanrasset, I realized members of my group were gradually overcoming fear. None of us sounded pessimistic as we progressively approached the border.

At around six in the evening that day, the barbarous driver, as Martin used to call him, asked us to rest once we arrived at another checkpoint. Some passengers were complaining about time, but the driver was careless about our complaint. Within forty-eight hours of our journey, my group and possibly some other passengers had adapted to the hot weather, the driver's stubbornness, and his barbs. We, the migrants, could identify ourselves by the looks on our faces, our outfits, or without baggage.

When we got to the next checkpoint {a small village} where the driver ordered us to rest, almost all the migrants—Anglophones and Francophones—sat under a very old tent while some bought food and water. In our various official languages, we talked about the pains we had gone through since we left our homelands and the expected and unexpected challenges ahead of us. As we were discussing, I had to move away from a chain-smoker. He wouldn't let me breathe fresh air because of the cigarette smoke. He smoked two to three sticks of cigarette at any checkpoint, and whole packets just for a night—the last person to sleep and the first to wake up. The driver banned him from smoking the moment he boarded the bus with smoke from his nostrils, mouth, and cigarette sticks. Within thirty seconds, a Malian boy almost distanced him. Sainabou hissed and left his presence until other members took notice of the smoke. He just coughed and walked away from us.

At that checkpoint, he was quelled by police because he couldn't afford to pay the officers. So, the police ordered the driver to leave him there. I heard his hoarse voice quaver as he begged the police to release him. I felt so bad, wishing I had the money to help. Our interpreter told us that the police would release him later. It's their habit to queers migrant's pitch when they noticed he/she is reluctant to pay. I was not sure about his nationality; he could be from one of the Francophone countries in West Africa, possibly Mali, Senegal, or Burkina Faso.

I can't remember all the checkpoints we crossed from Gao to the Malian-Algerian border, but I can remember we got to another checkpoint before we were finally betrayed by the driver and some other men. At the last checkpoint, before the driver made a U-turn, we met officers and migrants whose journey ended due to lack of money. Most of them have become adapted to the way of life of the inhabitants, helping officers to identify possible migrants and revealing to them how and where migrants hid their monies.

When we got in a queue, Emmanuel was the second person in the row. I heard Fatoumatta advising him to avoid standing in front of a queue. "On this journey, those who are always in the front face the strongest challenges."

One of the police officers looked at us querulously as if we had wronged him. He told us to make two lines: male and female. Emmanuel and the guy in front of him were asked to follow an officer to a tent. I thought they were taken there for questioning until our interpreter told us they were being searched thoroughly for money and other valuables.

Suddenly, Sainabou did queue-jumping quick in a flash and stood third from the front. The second in command became furious and ordered Sainabou to return to his previous position.

"Why did you do that?" Fatoumatta whispered.

"I wanted to be amongst the first few so I would reveal to you everything," Sainabou responded.

"They should have hurt you, Sainabou!" Fatoumatta said.

"Don't you see how bloody these guys are?" I added.

They didn't search us the female migrants, probably because there was no female officer to do so. We were just asked to hand over all the money we had. No female migrant was willing to do so, only the nervous one amongst us did. Franck, Emmanuel, and many other migrants on the bus were left with a penny. A Malian quibbled over his one five thousand francs. The officers took away almost one thousand and some hundred dollars from male passengers on our bus. Franck and Emmanuel lost two hundred and thirty dollars and some franc. It was another sad moment for us on board the bus.

"I don't even know how they knew we had money kept under the pads of our trainers." Emmanuel asked.

"Didn't you see the black stranded migrants who are there with the officers? They know how migrants keep hiding money," our interpreter said.

"You may be right. I saw one of them whispering to the officers and I thought he was begging for me," Emmanuel said.

Franck and Emmanuel had a spar, which didn't last long. Well, according to Franck, he warned Emmanuel to change the position of his money; they both shouldn't keep their money in a similar position. Our interpreter, who lost almost one hundred and fifty dollars at the hands of the officers, told Franck and Emmanuel they are sowing seeds that they shall reap. I was so concerned, that I had to ask Franck, Emmanuel, and our interpreter, what they were going to do when we got to Tamanrasset. I received no answer from anyone. They were not in the mood to answer any question that wouldn't bring back their monies, or maybe my question wasn't relevant to them.

The murmuring amongst the men didn't stop—not until we arrived at one point with a few men with guns dressed in police uniforms. It was at that moment I realized that all the remaining passengers on the bus were migrants. We were forcefully ordered to step out of the bus by the gunmen.

"Take your stuff out of the bus!" one of them ordered us.

I became panicky, just like the other passengers. We stepped out of the bus and made a queue. The gunmen in police uniform entered the bus and pretended to be searching. One of them stood at the door and told us to walk to Timiaouine, which is the border town, and then the driver made a U-turn and drove off.

Chapter 6

A new struggle began that very moment, and we had no other option but to come together and listen to one another. We were eighteen in number, as far as I could remember, and we were all from West Africa.

Our interpreter took the role of the leader, because he was fluent in English and French, and even some local tongues of Mali and the neighbouring countries. As we were discussing, some said to get to Timiaouine by foot would take us three days, some said two, others said one if we don't take a rest. We never bothered ourselves to ask our interpreter for his name until we overheard someone call him Ahmed. Ahmed implored us to start walking. "If we don't start walking now, the tediousness of the path to Timiaouine will still be in our minds," Ahmed said.

It wasn't a secret that many were fazed by the driver's action. Two women insisted they would return to the next village to seek advice, saying the path is very dangerous because of the ongoing conflict there. Ahmed and some other Malians reacted against their decision to return.

"Come, let's move further. Allah is with us! For the fact that you both want to get to the previous town safely is beyond the realms of possibility." Ahmed discouraged them, but the women were so determined to return, they both left us and went separate ways.

Grumbling and murmuring amongst us erupted, which Ahmed himself wasn't able to control. The truth is that only a few amongst us were optimistic about the journey. Our fate was unknown, our strength was weak, and what made us brave was never there.

Sainabou called Fatoumatta and me and showed us the only remaining bottle of water in her bag. Fatoumatta tapped us on our backs and told us to be strong. "You won't know you have wings until you jump from the cliff edge. Don't let the driver's action ravage your hopes," she said to us.

I knew for sure we may have to resort to living for hours or days without water. In that sandy and dusty desert, we were nothing but ordinary mortals.

In the desert, we walked in groups and told funny stories to comfort ourselves, but not those who were very nervous like me. I watched straight at the endless desert as I walked with my group. Only my heart could tell how I felt in that dark moment. Ahmed left his group and joined ours. "You guys are just a few; let me join you!" he said to us.

It was through our discussion that Ahmed told us he resided in Ghana for half a decade, then returned to Mali four years later, where he was re-trained as an Islamic teacher before he made the journey. He left his first and second wives and children at his late father's house in Bamako, Mali. He told us he was coming to make a way for them, as there is no hope in his country. Emmanuel, Franck, Sainabou, Fatoumatta and I listened to Ahmed keenly as he explained his family life and plight. Fatoumatta warned us earlier not to mention anything about our families to anyone for security reasons.

Ahmed told us he believes he will be rolling in money in Europe and make enough savings for his family. "I'm wondering how you guys knew my name. I can't remember I revealed it to any of you," Ahmed said to us.

I wanted to respond, before Fatoumatta interrupted me, saying, "We've ears, have we not?"

Ahmed smiled as he strolled tiredly on the dusty ground.

"Ahmed, are you tired already?" Sainabou asked.

"No! I'm saving my strength for days ahead!" Ahmed replied. "One day, two days, three days...we still don't know how long we might take before reaching our destination."

Franck, on the other hand, was reciting Bible verses.

"Is your friend nervous?" Ahmed asked us.

"You are both from Francophone country. You may ask him yourself!" Sainabou commented.

I sharply turned and looked at Franck with mystification. The grey-haired Ivorian boy was indeed nervous, sauntering like a walking time bomb. Ahmed told us a story about a faithful Malian Nabob, who was always furious when people worshipped him because of his money, but he likes hardworking and kind individuals. As the most generous person in his community—a humble type—he believed his family members and the public respected him so much because of his riches. Despite his being rich and influential, he could join the villagers to do public work and used his personal resources to improve the lives of others. As he grew older, he asked God to show him the child to whom he should bequeath his wealth. One day, he had a dream, where God told him to will his entire asset to his youngest daughter, whom the Nabob and some family members regarded as the laziest, wicked, and selfish amongst all his children. The dream became very disturbing to him since he once saw the girl as unfit to inherit his property because of what he had heard about her, and secondly because of her gender.

About a year later, he became very ill. As his health continued to depreciate, he was moved to a far community—a place where he had never been. In that village, he was taken to a wonderful magician's house set in an idyllic neighbourhood.

The location of the Nabob was kept from his children for almost three months. Throughout his stay in that undisclosed village, he always heard the villagers talking about a very generous and hardworking lady who visit them in the village often, but the lady never disclosed her identity to them. As the villagers continued talking about the lady, the Nabob became more eager to meet her in person and wished the girl was his daughter. The lady visited the village twice, giving the villagers some charity and helping them in their farm works, unbeknown to the Nabob. He became very furious at the villagers for failing to inform him when the lady was around. The Nabob and the chief of the village became mutual friends. After he totally recovered, the chief took him around and showed him some of the great things the lady had done for the people of the community. "Allow me to meet this angelic girl, and I will adopt her as my daughter!" the Nabob said to the chief. He immersed himself in trying to get the girl more than the villagers.

The lady visited the village two months after her last visit. While she was on the farm giving a helping hand to the farmers, the chief sent for the Nabob to meet the lady. Surprisingly, the lady happened to be the Nabob's youngest daughter, whom God spoke about. He immediately went down to his knees and asked God to forgive him for doubting his message. His youngest daughter finally inherited the nabob's assets.

I can't remember what Ahmed said about the dialogue between the girl and her father when they met. My legs were paining, so I paid more attention to them. He kept quiet when he noticed his story only had a few ears. He took out a biscuit from his pocket, shared it with us, and asked us to pray before eating it. Even though I was hungry, I didn't feel like eating anything. Even if I tried, I knew I wouldn't savour every bite of it.

Ahmed scuttled off to the other groups and shared his packet of biscuits. When he returned to us, there was nothing left with him. "So you've shared everything and have nothing for yourself, huh?" Fatoumatta said to Ahmed.

"It makes me feel so good in sharing the little I have with others," Ahmed responded.

"You have a heart of a true leader," Fatoumatta said.

"Thank you!" he accepted. Ahmed tried to steer the conversation away from his heart of generosity and asked me to tell him about life for foreigners in Sierra Leone.

"Sierra Leone is like any other sub-Saharan African nation—many Step ford wives!" I responded.

"How about Freetown. Is everything free there?" he joked.

I just looked at him and smiled. When the sun disappeared late in the evening, Ahmed asked all of us to stay closer. "We should leave no one behind!" he said.

I tried not to complain about my paining legs. Even if I did, I wouldn't have had any option but to keep walking. Emmanuel and Franck were at our heels. I turned around and watched them grab their hands. Ahmed advised us not to use light because it would endanger our lives. "Bad folks could see us from afar!" he warned us.

I was sandwiched between Sainabou and Fatoumatta. Hardly was I able to see the movement of others on my left and right-hand side. Since we started our journey in that dusty desert, my attention dragged me several times to a Malian or Togolese man, dark in complexion, who was drinking a liquid from a bottle swathed in very untidy wear. He would drink it when he thought nobody was watching. I observed him until he started strutting. Even though it wasn't bright, I could still recognize him in the dark. At around nine at night, he eventually staggered and fell on the sand. Ahmed and the others rushed to help him, only for them to smell alcohol evaporating from his mouth. "He's drunk!" Ahmed said and hissed. "Alcohol has taken control over him!"

We gathered around him as some men tried to make him stand. Ahmed said he knew there would be a delay, but not expected it to be that early, or from within.

While suggestions were pouring in, Fatoumatta took me out from the gathering and said, "I know that's the reason you were gazing at that drunkard, huh?"

I heard Ahmed speaking to the group, saying annoyingly that frustration and depression can make people annihilate themselves unknowingly. A well-built guy, proud friend to the drunkard, volunteered to carry him on his back. After about forty minutes, another guy assisted, until midnight when Ahmed suggested we take a rest.

After meditating for hours, I was—most likely—the last person to fall sleep. Very early in the morning, while almost all the Muslims were up for prayers, the drunkard, who had regained his consciousness, separated himself from us. He was fifty meters away from the group, eyes downcast! His muscled friend searched his small bag in front of us and poured the remaining rum on the sand before the drunkard joined us with shame written all over his face. No one mentioned his drunkenness the previous night. He looked gentle and humble when he was alcohol-free, notwithstanding after his conscience had pricked him. He apologized to us for his shortcoming.

After a five-hour walk that following morning, some people's bags became a burden to them. I saw some throwing away things they thought were unnecessary to them until they were left with nothing other than the stuff they put on. We ran out of water and food on the second day of our journey.

Two boys fainted under the hot burning sun, in the warm, dusty, and dry desert. Not too long after, they both stopped breathing. We struggled to save their lives, but we couldn't; one died after an hour, and the other a couple of hours later.

The tussled we had was whether we should leave the dead bodies buried or unburied or whether we should carry them to the next town and bury them with dignity as few suggested. Since the boy who first gave up the ghost had no relatives amongst us, we decided to dig a hole, about one foot deep, I think, and bury his corpse. The elder sister to the boy who died after insisted his brother should be taken to a nearby village or town and bury him respectfully.

"Who is going to carry it for you?" Ahmed asked her aggressively.

The woman turned around, probably to see whether she had support from other members of the group. When she noticed the majority frowned at her stubbornness, she finally decided, albeit unwillingly, and pleaded we pray over her brother's corpse. We did as she requested.

I can't tell you how the atmosphere was at that moment. There was nothing to pamper ourselves with, and many were not sure whether we would get to Timiaouine alive. Our human looks were fading, our strength dying, and our hopes becoming disheartened.

"Let's keep walking; we shall get there soon. Just don't give up. You've sacrificed your precious time and earnings to come this far, so don't give up guys!" I heard Ahmed talking in English and translated it into French, while Fatoumatta and I were helping Sainabou to do away with some stuff from her bag. In fact, she threw away everything except her panties. When we raised our heads, the others were almost seventy meters away from us. We tried not to bother ourselves to catch up with them. At least we were at the same pace.

While we were a distance away walking behind the others, Ahmed stood and waited for us, which brought pangs of hatred from some Malian ladies. Sainabou and Fatoumatta whispered in my ears in a very comic way. I just smiled and focused my attention on the woman who was crying—still dejected because of the loss of her relative. I couldn't hold my tears but shed them with the woman. I remembered Martin again, who died in pain, and Awa, who never even crossed the Senegalese border.

Fatoumatta used her grubby hands and wiped the tears from my eyes. "It's going to be okay! We shall glory when we get to Europe," she said to me.

Two Malian women turned and glowered at us. It was Sainabou who took notice of them and she called our attention to it. It was vivid; Ahmed himself took notice of the lady's glared looks at us. Sainabou asked Ahmed whether or not he was in love with any of them. He looked Sainabou straight in her eyes and said one of the ladies was his ex.

"Thought you said you were married with kids!" I said to Ahmed.

"Yes, I am!" he replied.

"But it's a sin for a married man to have a girlfriend!" I commented.

Suddenly, a woman fell; we all rushed and gathered around her. Sainabou took out her water bottle and pour the last drip of water into her mouth to save her. The woman guzzled down the drips from the bottle. Few others did the same to her. We stood there under the burning sun for almost two hours before the woman regained her strength, grunting as she stood. There were glum looks on all our faces. After we'd thought that the woman had finally regained her health, she collapsed and gave up the ghost almost immediately.

Her death caused panic in all of us, and our leader became confused. We just used the cloth tied around her waist to cover her face down to her body, then prayed and left her body unburied. Like a dagger to my heart, I felt the pain, and I never thought in my life I would have seen such nightmare in broad daylight.

After a few hours, I lost consciousness for hours. I saw myself on Fatoumatta's back later, heavily breathing. I lifted my head above Fatoumatta's back and counted us. *Fourteen remaining!* I said to myself, as I was crazed with fear of the unknown. I thought someone gave up when I wasn't myself amongst the craven migrants. It was only me at the back of someone, so I gently asked Fatoumatta to let me walk. "Are you strong enough to walk?" she turned and asked me.

"I think I am strong," I replied to her.

"You think! You saw what happened to the previous woman who insisted to walk, right?" Fatoumatta asked.

I went completely silent. Fatoumatta transferred me to Emmanuel's back, then to Franck, later to Sainabou, and finally to Ahmed. After the sun had disappeared, I quietly told Ahmed I was healthy enough to walk. Once I came down from Ahmed's back, Fatoumatta and Sainabou held me for some time. As the wilderness became darker, we walked closer to each other for safety, until midnight when we unwillingly rested, half-dead.

I had a dream—a very terrifying one. In that dream, I saw Emmanuel, Franck, Sainabou, and Fatoumatta, even Sabel Grace, and Alberta, tied to a giant tree. Behind me were some men heavily armed with different weapons. Five dead bodies were at my right-hand side gunned down by the armed men. There was a gun pointed at my head, and the man behind the barrel was possibly the leader of the men. The man urged me to shoot at my friends or lose my life first. As I was crying bitterly, the man behind me cocked the gun, coercing me to do or die.

Fatoumatta nudged me gently and said, "You are snoring heavily! Are you okay? Is someone pursuing you in your dream?"

I wanted to tell her about my dream, but it was traditionally bad to tell a dream at night. Aunty Mabinty told me many times that explaining scary dreams at night is weird. It was 2 a.m., I was sure—I couldn't sleep again until dawn.

Very early in the morning, another boy was found dead about thirty meters away from his friends. I noticed that it was the person I saw crawling gently in the dark. No Muslim prayed that morning, maybe because of the unpleasant thing that happened or because of no energy to pray. His corpse was also left unburied.

But before we left, Ahmed asked us all to pray for him in our different faith. Since we started our journey in the wilderness, Fatoumatta would frown whenever we were asked to pray over dead bodies. She grumbled to Ahmed not once but twice. She would say, "The dead don't need prayers; their good or bad deeds will follow them." She murmured incessantly and even told us that in case she died on the way, we shouldn't pray over her corpse. Sainabou told her to be careful about the things she wished for. We were left with no energy and hope. Despite all that, we were still moving, dragging our feet on the sandy ground with great distress and reproach.

My love for Fatoumatta and Sainabou was rock solid, even though throughout our journey they did some things that were not acceptable to me, like giving no attention to my opinion—especially on things that matter to us—or on something which led us into the wrong path of our journey. For instance, I told Fatoumatta to buy more water before we left Gao. She deliberately ignored my advice, probably because I was the youngest, or maybe because I made no financial contributions to our journey. I said the same thing to Sainabou, and she intentionally ignored me too. In Gao, while they were away negotiating with the agent, I saw potential migrants pouring water into huge containers. I also asked Fatoumatta to have a word with the old man who was trying to communicate something to us at the car park in Gao, I was again overlooked. I am certain he was trying to raise an alarm without been noticed by others.

As we were going, I thought about the dream I had, but I was so nervous to explain it to anyone. Fatoumatta, I knew, didn't like to hear negative news in the morning. The latest death of one of us was enough to ruin her day. No one would have had the appetite to listen to my dream—not sure they might forgive me. And walking for days without food and water, I wouldn't expect to see a hungry happy person amongst us.

Ahmed was looking very strong and enthusiastic as if he was bellyful. He walked closer to me and started talking about the ways sterile women were treated in his community in Mali. He said such women were least considered in society. I could hear his stentorian voice, not actually understanding all he said. The truth was nobody responded to him.

There was a sudden shout from behind. A lady from amongst the Malian group was bleeding profusely. As we rushed to help, the men were asked to back off. At first, I had no understanding of what was happening, because their conversations were in Bambara and French. I took a few steps back, gazing at the ring of women trying to help the lady. The people I tried to ask to update me about the lady's situation gave me deaf ears, so I stood there staring ignorantly apart from them. One hour later, under the angry sun, I heard some women crying. The woman died, Fatoumatta said to me. "No woman can survive such a harsh situation!" she said to me. I was nervous to ask Fatoumatta what really happened to the woman. I know it wasn't because of lack of food or water. I didn't believe lack of those basic necessities could lead to bleeding, and the gore came from between her legs. The women, with the support of some men, dragged the woman's body to the east and they covered her face with a wrapper which they untied from her waist, then we left.

It seems God left us to stew in our juice. Our smiles were stolen by the unpleasant things we saw every day in the desert. Sainabou held my right hand and said in a very weak tone and with a wry smile on her face, "We are alive! Aren't we?" I nodded my head, trying not to use my tongue that had not been used for hours. She avoided asking me whether I was okay, which was her usual question. She knew I wasn't.

I heard Ahmed telling Emmanuel and Franck that they shouldn't give up; we shall get to Timiaouine very soon. I sharply turned and looked at Ahmed; he went to me again and said the same thing. I wanted to ask whether it was a word of encouragement, or it was for real, but my tongue was too heavy to raise, and my attention span was getting shorter to listen to a long conversation. I wanted my dreams known to the others, and also to ask what led to the lady's bleeding. The strength wasn't there to do so. I prayed in my heart that our journey may not be a total write-off so that one day all would be written.

A few hours later, we came to a tree where some people asked Ahmed to let them rest or take a nap, but he insisted we should continue walking; the area where we were was a danger zone for humans. People, especially migrants, are easily kidnapped by militia groups. We all pleaded for him to give us thirty minutes rest to regain our lost strength, so he grudgingly agreed with us.

I admired Ahmed's unique leadership, even though he wasn't the oldest amongst us, even though he wasn't the bravest, even though he wasn't the strongest. He had the time to listen to everyone and was very decisive.

As we sat under the tree, Fatoumatta asked me to rest my head on her lap in case I wanted to take a nap. In spite of the fact that I did not have enough sleep the previous night, I wasn't feeling sleepy at all. Despite the long-distance walk, I needed no rest. Regardless of staying for days without food and water, I wasn't hungry or thirsty. Maybe I was, but my body stopped communicating with my brain. Ahmed took Sainabou to a distance away from us and had a word with her, while the two Malian ladies gave Sainabou an animus look. After their secret chat, Fatoumatta interrogated Ahmed. She asked him whether she was dating any of the Malian ladies that were moving with us and he became silent.

"Why did you ask?" Ahmed asked Fatoumatta with a smile. After seventy-two hours of walking in the wilderness, Ahmed's smiling and encouraging face never disappeared.

"It's not something to smile about!" Fatoumatta answered.

"She is my first date! We dated even before I travelled to Accra, Ghana, where I spent five years. I didn't clamp eyes on her when I returned to Bamako because I had been told she was forced to marry an Imam from another town. I was surprised to see her here making this journey with us," Ahmed stated.

"Seems she's still in love with you. Haven't you seen the way she makes eyes at you?" Fatoumatta said.

"I'm a married man now!" Ahmed stated. "My religion permits me to marry more than three wives, but I'm content with one. I don't need another, not even concubines!" he continued.

I thoughtfully listened to them but never butted in. Fatoumatta kept quiet. I know she didn't have the strength to continue the conversation with tireless Ahmed. I couldn't believe to see him buzzing around again strenuously to check on others sitting on the other side of the tree. At our back, I saw others stretching themselves out on the sandy ground under the sapling when I turned my stricken face.

Another thing about Ahmed was he was so conscious of time. After thirty-minutes promptly, he urged us to get going. "We shall have more time to rest," he gently said to us.

I watched others struggling to leave the ground so languidly, moving like a walking dead. Fatoumatta and I were the last two to stand up. She first stood and supported me with her hands.

For the first time, we saw Ahmed and his so-called ex chatting on our way going. I sharply turned my face to my left to look at Sainabou's reaction. Fatoumatta once whispered in my ear, when I lay my head on her lap under the tree, that it seemed Sainabou was completely infatuated with Ahmed. Sainabou focused her attention on Ahmed and his Malian ex-inamorata. After about twenty minutes, we finally got Sainabou's attention back. "Sainabou are you okay?" Fatoumatta asked.

She hissed and said she was okay. I acted as if I knew nothing. Sainabou tried to avoid looking at Ahmed and his Malian ex.

I tried to knuckle down on my mind. It is common for me to fight with my thoughts throughout our journey. I saw one guy kneeling to lace his shoes, and suddenly he dropped down. As he was breathing, with both eyes open, I heard him talking in a whispering tone, "Mon jambe! Mon jambe!"

Ahmed stood up and told us that the man is weak, and his legs could no longer stand. His's first two attempts to carry the man on his back were futile. They both fell down! His third attempt was successful and we walked behind them as we watched him staggered helplessly on the sand.

We were about eight hundred meters away from Timiaouine when we saw two pickup vans accelerating behind us. All of us gave the vans our attention, except a late twenties Malian who tried to run. He took noticed the vans belongs to militia groups, but we thought they were a rescue team from the Malian government. I felt invigorated after the three-day walk. As they got closer, about two hundred meters away from us, Ahmed dropped the man from his back and said, "They are a militia group!" By then it was too late.

No sooner had they got to us, one militia standing on the pickup van snipped down the Malian man who tried to escape, and they opened fire in the air. Fatoumatta pushed me to the ground violently and buried my face in the hot sand.

I heard the militias sniffing around us. One by one they tied our hands and faces with black pieces of clothes and brutally dragged us to the vans. I didn't know how many of us were on board the first van or who was there. I just believed one van couldn't accommodate all of us.

I whispered Fatoumatta's name twice but no response. I whispered Sainabou's name two times and no reply again. But when I called Franck's name once, the person tied next to me gently elbowed me and I assumed it was Frank. Right at that moment, I told God I never wished for it; I was only looking for peace and freedom in my life, and a decision to remain the way I came. As tears filled the black cloth tied to my eyes, I read the twenty-third Psalm in my heart and went silent, paying total attention to every sound around me. Nobody is safe in a vulnerable position, I know that. While the car was speeding up, the person next to me nuzzled up against me. *Is this Franck?* I asked myself. *Have I been a nymphet to him?*

The driver put his foot down for over an hour before he put the brake down and parked the van in a very quiet environment. We were dragged out again so aggressively like slaves and queued up under the hot burning sun. I felt somebody nudge me; it could be the same person who elbowed me in the van.

Suspiciously, they frisked us one by one and led us in front of a dilapidated warehouse. Our faces and hands were untied by a very huge disgusting black man, so black like coal. Fatoumatta was right in front of me, and at that moment I realized it was her who elbowed and nudged me. *How come she didn't answer when I called her name?* I asked myself.

We were ushered into the warehouse by another militia who was already there before we arrived, I think. A black skinned man, possibly their leader, called us one after another and gave us a cell phone to call our family members, telling them we've been held hostage. We were to pay a three-hundred-dollar ransom each with no negotiation.

Fatoumatta was among the first four people, and what was so scary was that all four of them received slaps before they could speak to their family members. It was a way to urge our family members to remit the money very quickly.

There were four people in the tiny room: a disgruntled lady, a young man who was their interpreter—possibly a Nigerian or Ghanaian—the slim dark guy who was their leader, and his bouncer standing by the door. Immediately after I entered the tiny and untidy room, the young lady and the bouncer came close to me.

"What's your name, my friend?" the interpreter asked me. He asked me the same question three times. I was so stubborn to reply to him until I received two slaps in a row from the lady next to me.

"I'm Miatta," nervously I replied.

"Where are you from, Miatta?" he asked me again.

"I'm from Sierra Leone," I answered.

"Put your hands up, Miatta!" the guy ordered.

As he was asking, he was interpreting our discussion to their leader, who relaxed on an old rocking chair, moving back and forth.

While my hands were up, the lady thoroughly searched me, and later put her left hand into my pants and took out the remaining dollars given to me by Fatoumatta. All of them in the room were beaming.

"Ha, ha, you think you are smart? Huh! Here in this building, even if you save money in your stomach we'll get it out. Now, Miatta, take that phone and call your family; let them know you've been held hostage and two hundred dollars the ransom. If the money is not remitted to us within forty-eight hours, get ready to say your last prayer!" the interpreter said to me.

I became completely terrified. I thought about what exactly I should say to him. Firstly, I wanted to tell them I left without telling my family. It should have made me more vulnerable to humiliation and dehumanization by the militias. I told them I lost both parents, and my aunt with whom I was staying had no phone. I'd no record of what happened to me after I made such a statement. I saw myself surrounded by Fatoumatta and the others some few hours later in a storeroom.

"What happened?" I asked them.

Chapter 7

Fatoumatta fetched water from a bowl that looks like a bird bath and offered me some. I rejected it at first. The metal cup was rusty and dirty; even the filthiest animal could not drink from it. Not even the courageous words from Fatoumatta could assuage my pains. She offered me the water from the same rusty cup again, and I rejected it the second time. "Do you want to die?" she whispered. "This liquid you have rejected twice has kept us alive until this time!"

Sainabou in whose lap I have laid my head was busy gazing at me. Fatoumatta drew nearer and presented me with the water the third time with tears running down her cheeks. "Please drink. I don't want you to die. You know how much I love you to bring you this far." She cuddled up against me. I closed my eyes and opened my mouth, as she gently poured out the stinking water in my mouth. The liquid tasted like chloroquine. A few minutes later, Fatoumatta smiled and said, "You see, you've drunk the poison, but you are still breathing." I had a shufti at the dirty cup; I couldn't believe I drank water from it.

As the others were discussing in a whispering tone, Ahmed shushed us, then we all focused on the door at our back. We heard the footsteps of one of the kidnappers walking toward us, but he just stopped halfway and returned. There was absolute silence in the granary, and at that moment I took notice of a clock whirring at the top righthand corner of the wall. I turned and gazed at it. It was in the evening, but it showed 2 p.m. I took notice again of whiplashes on Sainabou and Ahmed's bodies.

The kidnappers later came at dark, tied our eyes, and moved us to another location—not too far from Timiaouine.

Early in the morning, we could hear human voices from afar. After the Muslim migrants prayed, at around five in the morning, we all sat quietly pondering what to do next.

"Are they going to kill us?" I mused.

Sainabou interrupted me at that moment to tell me she didn't pray because there was no water to hold ablution.

"What's ablution?" I asked her.

Suddenly, one of the kidnappers bashed into the tiny room with a thunderous expression on his face. I became more worried, thinking it was time for us to be slaughtered. A few seconds later, another kidnapper showed up with a bucket of water. The bucket looked pretty decent compared to the previous one. He just dropped it at the door and left.

An hour later, a Malian guy suggested we get together and make a plan to escape.

"To where? We don't even know where we are at the moment," Ahmed commented.

"If we use our brains, we can think of a way out!" the man said. His name was Alieu—so dark and lanky! He was the most jovial amongst us, despite his broken English, yet we were able to understand him.

"These guys have guns! Have you ever used one, or you are just a greenhorn like me?" Ahmed asked, and slightly turned and interpreted the question he asked him.

All of us gazed at him as we waited on his answer. Alieu just smiled and said, "We're all gunmen if a gun is the only thing to freedom."

Some people giggled at his answer, except our group, which includes Franck and Emmanuel. We had to wait for Ahmed to translate his words for us. It wasn't a juicy reply to me or anyone member of my group.

Before the day ended, the kidnappers had received an enormous amount of money from our relatives. Fatoumatta got her fiancé to remit my ransom. His name was Joseph Williams, an Aku from the Gambia. Alieu's relatives turned him down, accusing him of betraying the family in a shameful way, saying let him be on his own and shoulder his own cross.

The following night, our faces were tied again and we were moved to another location. That very night, the kidnappers took Alieu away, and since that day, I never set eyes on him again. I can't tell whether he was killed or set free since the kidnappers never returned to us.

We embarked on a journey to Timiaouine in darkness, and at around four in the morning, we were rescued by the Algerian border guards that took us to Timiaouine. Amongst the things I left behind in the desert, my father's note was wrapped in a black and red sleeveless dress, and Martin family's contact.

We met some other migrants in Timiaouine, who had been stuck because of several vital reasons. Some were there waiting for their family members to remit money from home to continue their journey, or pay their way back. Some couldn't pay their way to continue or to return to their country of origin, and their families were not ready to send them any fund. Amongst them were two Sierra Leonean ladies, named Mamusu Jawara and Isha Kebbeh. Mamusu was around her mid-twenties and twenty weeks pregnant. She became pregnant after she was gang-raped at knifepoint by some Malians in Bamako-Mali. On my first night with her, she told me she couldn't continue her journey because of one of the negative impacts of rape, so she was volunteering to work as a maid to get food to eat. Her family couldn't send money for her because her stepmother, who was the breadwinner of her family, suddenly died of a heart attack the very day she departed Freetown. She was sleeping in a deserted building with other stranded migrants; over one hundred, I think. We had no money with us, but if we did, I should've given it to her right away.

The story of smugglers conspiring with armed robbers, kidnappers, or militias to extract money from migrants is very common in that area. Mamusu advised us not to stay in Timiaouine, as it is not a congenial working environment, especially for migrants from sub-Sahara Africa. We should do all we can to get to Tamanrasset.

We got stock in Timiaouine for several days until Fatoumatta's boyfriend remitted another fund for her, which was only enough to take us to Tamanrasset. Isha Kebbeh, the other Sierra Leonean, who never told us she was six weeks pregnant, decided to join us.

I watched tears running down Mamusu's cheeks the day we left Timiaouine. "Do not forget me when you arrive," she said to us.

Spending almost six nights with her and the other stranded migrants at the abandoned building gave me a different view of life; especially the hard truth. I hugged and pecked her more than two times in her dusky yellow dress, and she politely asked me to take good care of myself. Today, I can remember what she told me the very first day we thronged into that abandoned structure. "Not all who pray will see Heaven." I can't believe she woke me up when the whole block was asleep just to make such a proverb. She said her boyfriend, who first made the journey, was throttled by unknown militias. She left behind her first child in Freetown, hoping when she arrived in Europe, life would be uplifting. "Sometimes I wish I had aborted this baby; it has become a stopping sign to me!" She said that two times. I deliberately refused to translate it to Fatoumatta and the others; it could be a disturbing saying to them, not a throwaway even to me.

As we embarked on another tedious journey from Timiaouine to Tamanrasset, as frail and unhealthy as I was, my group never left me in the dust. I thought of the bunch of migrants sleeping in that dilapidated building. And Mamusu told me there was more than three times the number we met there, but they eventually dwindled due to many whys and wherefores. In fact, she wasn't the first, neither the second nor the third pregnant migrant woman to have dwelled in that building. The first one died of torture, the second died of hunger, and the third perished of an unknown disease. "And what am I going to die of?" Mamusu asked as she was on a knife edge. She grinned feebly at me. At my age, based on all that I have seen, the hazards I had inevitably faced, and the dangers I was going to face, I quite understand the troubles behind her grin.

We were all aware of the brutal life for migrants in Libya—the major gateway for Africans to enter Europe. We were also conscious of the hellish detention, the harsh human trafficking, and brutal death for migrants in Tripoli and Sabratah, but our determination to continue our journey was greater than our discouragement to stay or return home. We hoped for a better life, like those who made it to Europe before us, those in known and unknown detention centres in Libya, and those that died trying. Despite the weird stories we heard from other migrants we met on our journey, and despite the threats from inhabitants on our way or the unexplainable tribulations, I never heard, not a single time, a member of our group talking about returning home, neither spoke fear. We were just going like rolling stones pushed from a mountain top.

Fatoumatta, Ahmed, Sainabou, Emmanuel, Franck, and I, who were once captives, were able to travel to Tamanrasset, joined by Isha, who received some money from her relative in Freetown. Ahmed got financial help from his uncle in Timiaouine. What made me cry at that point in time was when I mistakenly called Martin instead of Franck, which made the whole team go silent.

We got a pickup truck to Tamanrasset that very morning. Next to me was Ahmed. He asked me the funniest question again, whether everything is free in Freetown. I knew he wanted me to smile once more, after all the tough things we had gone through. Indeed I grinned and said, "Not absolutely. In Freetown, the rich live as if they are poor and the poor as if they are rich." I made him beam too.

"I just wanted to drive away from the demon of depression in us," Ahmed said. Ahmed, who once called me Mia correctly, pronounced my name Miatta. He told me he had listened attentively to Mamusu and Isha—how they say my name. Fatoumatta and Sainabou were still calling me the old way. Isha was in complete silence. There was no sign of regret in her either—she just smiled at me.

Sainabou and Fatoumatta were at the back discussing in Wollof. Since Isha and I were the only people that can speak Krio, she informed me about her pregnancy, and I was embarrassed. "Were you raped?" I asked her.

"No, I wasn't!" she replied.

"Were you pregnant before you left Sierra Leone?" I asked.

"No!"

"How? When?" I anxiously asked.

"You won't understand!" she replied to me.

"Understand what? Are you another version of Mary?" I asked with curiosity.

The expression on my face and my tone of asking gave a cause for alarm. I never expected Isha to respond to my question, and she never did until an hour later when we had a breakdown under the hot burning sun. Ahmed, who was very observant, knew Isha wasn't totally okay, so he hefted the spare tire from the back of the vehicle and asked Isha to sit on it. I sat next to her on the other side of the tire. "Can you please tell me what really happened?" I whispered.

"Oh, oh, Miatta! I shall explain that in detail when we get to Tamanrasset," she responded.

"Well, my anxiousness won't fade away until you feed my ears with the food they need!" I said.

She just beamed at me.

"You will become hefty before we get to Europe," I commented again.

Isha scoffed and said, "I left Sierra Leone some fourteen months ago and travelled to Guinea Conakry to join the others. Conakry was our meeting point, and we got there the same day. The Sierra Leonean lady who accommodated us and fed us ended up hiring some bandits that robbed us. I lost almost a thousand and some hundred dollars in one night. I worked like a slave for almost a year to raise that money, and asked my family to sell half of the only piece of land left behind by my late father. The land was owned by both my siblings and I. Returning home empty-handed was a disgrace and a burden to me, thus, I was inspired by others to jump into prostitution for a year to raise the required amount I needed to get to Europe. I was fooled by a fool not to use a condom the night before we departed Conakry—a rich dude—and he paid me five times the money I demanded from men for a night. That's what got me pregnant. The most painful thing that happened to me again was losing the money I got from prostituting to some idiots on the road."

I wanted to ask her why she didn't return home, therefore I asked myself the question first. I couldn't answer it, because it didn't have an answer.

"My pregnancy is still very early, so I will try all I can to get to France. In this penurious life I have found myself, I would hate to see my unborn child live it," Isha continued, speaking in Krio.

Suddenly, there was a perceptible change in her voice, which made her a centre of attraction. When she came too aware that she had drawn the attention of the others, she went completely silent. Fatoumatta, who sat by Isha's righthand side, told her tears mean

125

nothing to any of us, as the inexorable horror is something we freely accepted ourselves.

"We have lost probably everything and disrespected our family by leaving without their approval. Some did deceitful things to raise the required amount to make this journey. To many it's unacceptable because they can't see the dreams in our minds or the horrific parts of our lives. If we think about all we have lost and endured, and the expected, we are going to cry out all our tears all at once. So I don't worry much about being abducted, ill-treated, or arbitrarily hurt. Even though we acknowledge it, we don't anticipate it happening to us, but our anticipations can't skip the realistic side of the path," Fatoumatta said, as she snuggled to Isha and gently rubbed her palms on her back.

"It's hurting; try not to feel it!" Ahmed commented.

There was no spare tire, so we waited for hours for replacement under the burning sun. Two passengers almost fainted, and a year-old baby lost its life five hours later. As the sun was setting, there was a tussle amongst passengers on whether we should wait for the tire to be replaced or trek.

"It is a walk that will take us more than twenty-four hours, and it's very risky," Ahmed said to us.

The perennial problem of trekking from town to town became part of us. We finally decided to continue the journey on foot. There was no way the driver was going to get the tire replaced in the shortest possible time and returning was worse than continuing. The driver sniggered at us for some time as we walked away.

We trekked from that scorching desert to Tamanrasset within twelve hours. Besides the toddler that we lost when we first broke down, we lost five more migrants: an early forties man, two women—including Isha Kebbeh and two beautiful girls—about eight others left behind weak and unhealthy. It was common for dying migrants to contact numbers to reach out to their relatives. "Please, call my mother when you can tell her I couldn't make it to Europe!" a young migrant, possibly from Liberia, hopelessly asked of me. Isha asked such a favour from me also.

We arrived in Tamanrasset at noonday the following day and joined other stuck and languished migrants like us. I listened to a lot of disheartening and painful stories, one from a 38-year-old man and his family from Senegal, who were arrested by a contingent of Algerian police officers and took him to Tamanrasset with almost hundreds of other working migrants and their families. Some of them were first detained for several days before they were taken to Tamanrasset. What I heard pricked my soul that very moment.

We spent our first night in Tamanrasset on a construction site. Sainabou, Fatoumatta, and I slept under a tipper truck. Ahmed, Franck, Emmanuel and some other Malians were under a caterpillar, others were outside a warehouse, and some in out-dated trucks. We slept on the bare sand on our backs. Before saying goodnight, Ahmed and the others spent time with us; we sat between the heavy trucks discussing our next moves. Fatoumatta uttered some words of admiration to Ahmed, but he was uncomfortable with praises from any of us. He dodged responding to a lot of thanks and gratitude from many who benefitted from his leadership role. I slept on Sainabou's lap while they were discussing.

At night, I heard voices, possibly from some of us, so I nudged Fatoumatta to wake up. Fatoumatta in turn elbowed Sainabou. We

127

attentively listened to them for over an hour before they sauntered away. After they left, Fatoumatta told me she was told the place was used by harlots at night. The construction workers, mostly Algerians, would hire sub-Saharan male migrants to get stranded female migrants to be paid cheaply for sex. They were doing homosexualism too, especially to young boys. Since I heard that from Fatoumatta, I couldn't sleep until the sun came up.

In the morning, we had unskilled jobs at the construction site; major jobs are precisely for males. When one of the workers at the site arrived in the morning, she was very furious at the security guard for letting us in, but when the rayiys, which means boss, arrived at the site, he denounced his workers' behaviour towards us. At ten in the morning, we ate one of the best meals since we left Senegal. It was couscous, meat, and some vegetables. I became very weak and indolent after the meal, but there was no choice but to work fervently. At the end of the day, the boss told us he would be paying us on a weekly basis. His English language wasn't that good, and his accent was hard to comprehend, but we did manage to understand him. His decision of paying us on a weekly base didn't go down well with me and some other migrants. I whispered to Fatoumatta about my disapproval; she just turned and frowned at me. "Wouldn't you see grown-ups didn't say anything? Here we listen to their tones and dance to their tunes," Fatoumatta said to me.

The boss called Ahmed an automaton and promised to compensate him at the end of every week, which made more enemies for Ahmed. Something arose between him and another Malian migrant the evening the boss left the site. It was a little tussle, but it turned out to be a brutal fight between them. Ahmed overtly accused the other Malian migrants of using Malian female migrants as sex workers. He also accused him of taking advantage of them. It seems we were not the only ones that were awake the previous night; Ahmed and a few others were awake too. The argument continued for over thirty minutes before they got back into their shells. The Malian guy who had a fight with Ahmed left the site and went away. We were told the guy had been in Tamanrasset for over fourteen months before we arrived there. So, he was well-known around the community for turning female migrants into sex workers and was suspected of working with some Algerian kidnappers.

I am pretty sure it was because of some of the unpleasant things Ahmed heard about his debauched fellow Malian that he became paranoid. His countenance completely changed; one could tell Ahmed was somehow troubled. He complained many a time he didn't like a person in debauchery practices. "Could you believe he was in Libya in the death row of the former Libya leader, Col Gaddafi?" Ahmed said nervously. His debilitating state wasn't encouraging at all.

As we gathered together around late in the evening, we were joined by two other female migrants from Guinea Conakry. They were both looking for safety where safety could not be found. The migrants from Francophone countries had a conversation with them; painfully, we had a similar experience traveling from our home countries to Tamanrasset—raped and tortured because their families couldn't pay their ransom. How did they manage to escape? None of them could explain it. "C'est un mystere," one of them said. When we cocooned under the machines, Ahmed crawled and joined us for a chat. He expressed bitter feelings about the way our fellow

Africans, specifically sub-Saharan Africans, were abusing their kids. With shivering hands, he secretly handed over five hundred dollars to Fatoumatta for safekeeping.

"Ahmed, you have this amount of money and you are still here? This sum of money can take you over the sea!" Fatoumatta whispered to him.

"It's not enough for us," Ahmed said.

"For us, how do you mean?" Fatoumatta asked.

"Me, you and your sisters," he replied in a quieter tone.

All of us gazed at him for almost thirty seconds before he continued. "We're all one family now, and I can't leave you guys behind to take your last breath on this journey. We shall all get to our dreamland together.

Ahmed told us he didn't trust the two Guinean ladies who arrived after the brutal guy left. "They have got a cod Guinean accent," he said to us as he crept back to his sleeping place.

We were left speechless under the truck. I was touched by what he said and felt guilty for misunderstanding support for an infatuation. I was so guilt-ridden that I couldn't watch him creep back. Sainabou broke the silence by calling Ahmed a kind-hearted and genuinely humble man. "So, all the work he's doing here is to help us raise our money?" Sainabou asked.

The next morning, we were up early, as usual, and we got a piece of astounding news from outside that two migrants were found dead in an abandoned garage not too far from where we were. Some said they died of hunger, and others said they were both raped to death, but the fact that death took place to other migrants kept us worried. The news didn't sound surprising to Ahmed. He told us to be careful and vigilant, especially at night, because what we heard wasn't new to his ears. "We have migrants dying every day in unknown locations here in this country, so we should act like death is coming tomorrow!" he said. I went back again into an abyss of fear.

On the third night, Emmanuel and Franck joined us under the old truck and spent the night there with us. In the morning, Franck suffered a crick neck which he claimed to be from a terrible nightmare he had overnight. A pious born-again Christian like Emmanuel doesn't like to hear Franck complaining about witches and wizards, because to him, they are powerless. Due to the complex he had over Emmanuel, he went completely silent. Not too long after, he collapsed and took his last breath so suddenly.

Franck's death never affected Emmanuel's strong will to continue his journey. For a couple of days, he went completely sad, and not until after three days did he show our boss how strong-minded he was. Though he was a strong man, so proud to say that the loss of his closest buddy couldn't let him stand the tears, I saw him cry bitterly behind the outdated caterpillars many a time. He gave me a stern warning not to tell anyone, but I did to Fatoumatta and Sainabou. Nobody dares encourage him to return home. In fact, he had no contact with Franck's family.

During our journey, it was common for migrants to deny knowing dead folks, despite the cordiality that once existed between them. The authorities on the way usually ask close friends or relatives of the deceased to return home with their corpses. Sometimes, unless coercive force is used before, friends or relatives would take up the responsibility. I was the youngest on the construction site until a woman from Liberian went there with her eight-year-old son who died a week later. The boy was seriously sick even before they arrived from Bamako; he sobbed loudly a whole night before he finally gave up the ghost.

On the eve before the day we hoped to be paid, the Malian-Algerian guy who had a confrontation with Ahmed went to the construction site at night with some Malian harlots and some of his gang members to run his usual business. Ahmed wasn't asleep; he sat right in front of a caterpillar reciting some surah. When they entered the property, they made a deal with the gateman, who was also an Algerian Malian, and then the girls and some ready men went to the warehouse. Sainabou, Emmanuel, and I were not asleep also. I heard their voices but couldn't understand what they were discussing. While he and his youngsters were outside waiting, they noticed Ahmed was sitting a distance away from them. As he swaggered towards Ahmed with his stern face, I immediately told the others about the perils. He had a tough tussle with Ahmed before he took out a dagger and stabbed him three times. He first stabbed him on his neck and twice on his stomach and ran away—the rest of his boys fled with him. We rushed to help Ahmed only for us to find him taking his last breath. Due to the shout, the gateman ran out of the warehouse and found Ahmed on the ground motionless and bleeding profusely. Fatoumatta asked me to stand behind his back and close my eyes. Another tussle broke out between the prostitute and the men. They never wanted to pay the ladies because of the incident that took place.

The patron became very furious at what happened and promised to find the bane. He called us all together and asked if anyone knew Ahmed. All of them denied knowing him except me. After gazing at me for almost a minute, he realized I couldn't handle his corpse alone, so he gave us each six thousand five hundred Algeria dinar, which was about forty-two Euros, and drove us out of the site. According to some others, he was a good man, otherwise he would have held us there until the Algerian Police arrived, but he let us scarpered.

We sheltered with other stranded sub-Sahara Africans in an abandoned construction site with a very big warehouse. Nothing like death scared the shit out of us, and sceptical that not all of us will make it to Europe. There, for the first time, we the stranded migrants contributed and had a banquet. It was from another migrant there at the warehouse we knew that one hundred and fifty dollars will take us to Libya. Immediately, Fatoumatta called us together and shared the information with us. With the money Ahmed left behind, plus the one given to us by the site manager, we had enough to get us to Libya.

But how? I asked myself. There was no bus, no comfortable ride from Tamanrasset to Libya. The only available means of transport were pickup trucks, and we couldn't access those pickup trucks without the help of smugglers.

Not too long after, we were introduced to two smugglers to traffic us to Libya. He told us there was no direct ride to Libya; his plan was to take us to Debdeb, an Amenas District, Illizi Province, Algeria, the border with Libya, for the sum of one hundred dollars. Frankly, I was agitated about the route. My thought was to get direct transport to Tripoli which Fatoumatta told me was impossible. I had to spend minutes agonizing about the journey again. We concluded the arrangement, and they were to pick us up at the warehouse early the next morning.

While we were returning to the warehouse after seeing the smugglers, Sainabou said the smugglers acted like imbeciles probably because they were gazing at her big breasts. She didn't get any response from us until when we arrived home. "Is it because they were looking at your breasts?" Fatoumatta asked Sainabou, but her question was ignored. "And your breasts look so immaculate, what would you expect?" Fatoumatta said again. Her comment made Sainabou smile.

In the evening, the Nigerian man whom migrants used to pay to make a call home arrived at the warehouse. Fatoumatta called her boyfriend to inform him about our next moves. And for the very first time since I ran away from my aunt's house, I thought about phoning her to say hi. But besides the U.S. code, I could only remember the first six digits. I later remembered the two of the last three digits, so I guessed the last digit. The guy who picked up my call became very furious at me for asking for my aunty he never knew. What made it very disturbing was calling him at the wrong time. My conscience pricks me that very moment that I may have disturbed someone, so I quietly gave the phone to the man and watched Fatoumatta pay the unnecessary bill.

The night before we departed to Debdeb, a migrant from Liberia, possibly around 34-years, died of heart attack. We knew the police would come to investigate his death, and in doing so the majority would be arrested. I am glad the smugglers went to pick us up early in the morning before the police arrived at the scene.

Honestly, I thought traveling from Tamanrasset to Debdeb was just an hour's drive, but it isn't. It took us two hostile days before we finally got to Debdeb. The truck was filled and congested with sub-Sahara migrants. We had a few unhealthy ones in the truck, and two of them died of asphyxia, hunger, and thirst. I was unconscious for hours also. According to some migrants who were acquainted with the roads, we were told the smugglers took irregular routes to avoid any contact with the forces. Well, my group survived the hot and airless drive.

Chapter 8

We arrived in Debdeb, very unhealthy, late in the afternoon two days later. We were taken to another construction site not too far from a large mosque with white paint. The dizziness in me wouldn't let me say a word for hours after we arrived. There were other migrants present there and they were predominately males, who used the unfinished building as a workplace and as a residence at the same time. Fatoumatta, Sainabou, and I were the only females amongst them.

With the advice of some migrants, we spent the first week at the construction site, and also worked there for a very low wage: first because we are females, secondly, because we had no experience. Not all areas in the building women are allowed to be, and not all work we were allowed to do. When I compared the wage given to the male workers, it was three times ours, and the worst of all, the Algerian workers speak indiscreetly to us. Many a time, they spat on our faces when we made mistakes while working.

The first night we slept in the unfinished building, we slept on old unwanted mats and cards used by migrants who were there before us. We were told later that the dusty room with uncovered windows they asked us to occupy was considered a bit of bad luck because two migrants had died there. Even when we were told about the horrible deaths that had taken place, we were left with no choice but to make ourselves comfortable. It wasn't new, for we are used to making a home in hell.

The first morning after Fatoumatta and the other Muslim migrants had prayed, I asked Fatoumatta and Sainabou what our next step was. I didn't know they both discussed it while I was sleeping, so they gave me the same answer. Fatoumatta had ideas on how we would get to Sabratah, from there to Tripoli, but her idea was inchoate, so we had to give her time for it to be developed; probably after making research on the migrants we met there.

One day, I was outside the building when the contractor came in with his wife and son. They only spent an hour and left. Immediately after they drove off, I saw his wallet next to where he parked his car. I was the only one around. I majestically walked and picked up the wallet. In there were about six-hundred-dollar notes and some dinars. I rushed and showed the wallet to members of my group who were inside the damp room lie-down. Tussled arose amongst us on whether we should give the wallet back to the contractor or see the money as a gift or help from God. "Sometimes Allah will use someone's misfortune as wealth for others. He knows what his servants are going through, that's why he had used greedy person's wealth to help us the needy," Sainabou said.

"At this trying time, God will forgive us!" Emmanuel said quietly.

Fatoumatta and I were totally against the idea of keeping the man's wallet. She asked that we should give it back to him. "If he asked!" Sainabou interrupted. "We are about to make the biggest mistake in our journey. Allah will forgive us if it's a sin!"

We forgot about the wallet when we heard shouting and crying at the back of the building. A disgruntled migrant worker had jumped from the second floor of the unfinished building and died instantly. After the traumatic incident, that very night, I was the last person to sleep. I sat and spoke to myself for hours. In the morning, I boldly told them I would give the wallet back to the man with or without their approval. "My conscience will lay a guilt trip on me, and it will leave nothing but a stigma in my mind," I said to them. They were all very surprised because I had never been that bold enough to speak to them since we met.

I guilelessly handed the wallet to the man when he showed up at the site the following day, and in return, he gave me a modest amount of money. Sainabou reviled my action, including the modest appreciation given to me by the man. I felt good; my soul was revivified right at that moment, and I was touched when he told me thanks. Sainabou and Emmanuel looked saturnine, which made me nervous to look at them twice.

One Friday, Fatoumatta convinced me to pray with them in a little corner about two hundred meters away in the big building. It was a place in the unfinished building they preserved for women and girls residing in the building to pray. At first, I was reluctant to go, but I later agreed after convincing myself with a few reasons: firstly, I wanted to pray in the Muslim way at least once, secondly, I won't die if I go there, and thirdly, staying alone without them would've been riskier.

I overheard some men talking about me having sexy breasts. After prayers, I asked Fatoumatta an unanswered question which she ignored many times. Two men walked behind to meet me specifically;

they softly spoke to me and encouraged me to visit again. "How did they know I am new here?" I asked Fatoumatta.

"Your barrage of questions will never end!" she responded to me. All the others laughed.

On our way to our exposed room, Fatoumatta and one Algerian man stood chatting on the pavement. I tried to hang around them, not only to eavesdrop, but also I feel more protected being around Fatoumatta. However, she blinked her right eye. I got the message and left, walking quickly to join the others. Nobody said a word to me until we got to the place we called home. I knew they were still hurt because I gave the wallet to the man. And nobody was more hurt than Sainabou, who often called me a young fool. Even though I felt guilty that I betrayed their dubious plans, I felt prouder that I handed over what wasn't mine.

Fatoumatta returned about half an hour later and told us she had met an honest smuggler who was ready to traffic us to Sabratah-Libya for one hundred and fifty dollars, and that was when the issue about the wallet arose again. Fatoumatta and Sainabou had a very tough confrontation in Wollof, which kept us gazing at them, surprisingly. Sainabou had always expressed how much confidence she had in Fatoumatta, but supporting my moves to hand over somebody's property back to him made her see Fatoumatta as a weak leader. They didn't argue in any other language except in Wollof. Neither Fatoumatta nor Sainabou could tell me what they may have said to each other, no matter how hurtful it may have been. Sometimes Sainabou would frown her face for hours after tussling with Fatoumatta, but she never extended her madness to me.

The constructor, whom we called patron, unexpectedly came to the building site to get a few things done. While he was talking to one Liberian migrant, he noticed two migrant workers were missing, so he ordered the boys to search around for them. Unfortunately, one of the two missing dudes was found dead. The following day, he returned to notify us that we should quit the unfinished building every day after work for security reasons. As we were working, about three hours later, the boss met Fatoumatta and me on one of the balconies. He called to know whether I had a place else to stay beside the unfinished building.

"No sir!" I responded.

"Did you travel alone?" he asked again

"No!" I answered.

While he was asking, Sainabou joined us.

Right in the presence of Sainabou and Fatoumatta, he asked me to give him the names of the folks that I travelled with. He returned later and told me he had made provision for us to stay in the neighbourhood about three blocks away from where we were, and a special meal would be served to us every day until the building project ends or we decided to continue our journey.

For three days consecutively, Fatoumatta waited at the usual point to reach an agreement with the smuggler he met, but alas and alack, the guy never showed up. It kept Fatoumatta worried, even though there were other notorious smugglers around town. Until now, I don't know why she had a special interest in that specific fellow. Sainabou asked her once in front of me, but she replied in Wollof. "Lajumala." What made it funny was the way Sainabou sidled up to me and said something in my ears. I smiled, and Fatoumatta hissed and left the room. She returned after with a smiling face with some bananas in her hands, but I earlier thought she was mad at us. After she shared the bananas among us, she sat us down and said, "Let's don't forget we left our countries to travel to our dreamland. Let don't forget we are still on the journey. This country or town shouldn't be a comfort zone for us. You may be wondering why I was so worried because that smuggler didn't show up as he promised; the guy honestly told me the challenges ahead, which you could hardly hear from any smuggler."

I got lost in the shuffle while she was talking until I was pushed by Sainabou. "Miatta, are you okay?" she asked me.

On our next visit to the meeting point, Fatoumatta was told that the smuggler she had been yearning to see was caught in incestuous sexual intercourse with his first cousin. Since incest is forbidden, he had been taken to Tamanrasset. Sainabou told us he visualized it weeks earlier that the guy was in a more dubious act besides smuggling. According to Sainabou, her great-grandparents, both from the parents' sides had sibyls. Since her generation never had one, she claimed to have had a little portion of it. Fatoumatta never liked someone telling her what would happen, so Sainabou's ancestral inheritance was nothing but trash to her. Despite the little tussles between Fatoumatta and Sainabou, or anyone else in my group, I never disdained any.

When we returned, we were told Emmanuel had left for Libya. Fatoumatta immediately rushed to the room.

In her absence, I wondered what urged her to rush into the room.

Is Fatoumatta suspecting them of a dubious act? I asked myself.

Sainabou left my presence and followed Fatoumatta to the room. I rebuked the thought that a gentleman like him would turn out to be a thief, but indeed he later proved to be. Fatoumatta came out screaming that Emmanuel had stolen our savings. I pretended at first as if I didn't hear such terrible news, which was something my ears never anticipated for. It felt like all my senses had been deactivated. I quietly sat on the floor and relaxed my body to the wall.

The following morning, our boss, the contractor, together with his wife, arrived at our apartment to pick us up, which is something he never did. All of us were surprised. What made it strange was seeing his wife joining him that morning. They were glamorously dressed. The woman was in a green haik dress which covered her from head to toe, and her husband with loose-fitting trousers of the same colour.

About one kilometre from the building, in a very quiet location, he pulled over. After asking us several questions about how we like our new temporal home.

"Guys!" he called our attention. "Seventeen years ago, my schoolmate became homeless. I decided to shelter him, even though I didn't have much, but I was able to share with him all that I had: my tiny apartment, my old-fashioned wear, my tasteless food, and many more. In that apartment where I was, I had my savings, which I had saved to go to university in France some months later. This friend of mine homed in on my long-time savings and disappeared. It was ten years before I was able to get eyes on him. If you were me, what would you do to that friend if you have the opportunity to meet him again?

I paused. Was the question directly to me or for us? I quietly turned to my left to watch the reactions of Fatoumatta and Sainabou.

"Are you guys okay?" he asked us again.

"Yes, we are!" I answered. "I will forgive him," I continued. I don't know how the sentence came out of my mouth. I was already furious at what Emmanuel did to us. The contractor turned to my two friends and asked them whether they agreed with what I said and they both nodded.

"Perfect!" he said.

As he was whispering to his wife, the thought that came to my mind was to see Emmanuel arrested so we could get back our money to continue our journey and also plead for their release. We needed the money, and we needed it desperately.

The contractor told us that Emmanuel had been incarcerated at the police station. He handed over to us the money he stole from us. We were struck with surprise. All the questions that ran to my mind at that moment were the same in Fatoumatta and Sainabou's minds, they confessed it to me later.

How the contractor knew about their havoc, how he was able to locate them, and how he knew about the actual amount stolen by the boys was a mystery. At that very moment, he connected us with one agent, and on that fateful day, we departed to Libya.

We left at midnight with other migrants from central and west Africa. I cried while sitting between Fatoumatta's legs, as she sat on the tailgate of the pickup van. We were forced by the driver to put on a traditional Islamic headdress, possibly to disguise ourselves. No covering of the head, no passengers. It matters not whether you are a Christian or Muslim, you must dress like a traditional Muslim being.

Just an hour after we left Debdeb, a very arrogant migrant from Guinea Conakry ordered Fatoumatta to sit on the floor because she was a woman. He forcefully pressed her to sit on the floor panel. When he took notice that Sainabou was a girl too, he pushed her again and asked another boy to take her space on the tailgate.

Down there was another lady who was reciting verses from the Quran over and over again. One could hardly take notice of the gender, unless through her voice. We disguised ourselves—not because we wanted to hide our identity but to prevent ourselves from the diseases that come through the dust. As we were certain of Europe, you could tell from our faces how hankered we were for a better life. I was seeking freedom, and to me, freedom means a better life.

In the dead of night, we smelled trouble in the darkness. I saw death in worries, and I saw no hope. When I started praying, I felt God was far away from me. Aunty Mabinty once told me God doesn't answer the prayers of defiant people, and I disobeyed my aunty for my good and was ready to meet anything ever after. I felt forced to cherish the perils, otherwise, I would have died before I face death itself.

That same night, some migrants were left behind because of disagreement with smugglers; some fell off the truck, including the arrogant Guinean boy who pushed Fatoumatta, and two others died before dawn. For those who were left behind, of course, there was no rescue mission for them. We picked up a teenage girl from a nearby village, whose name I couldn't even pronounce, but that same girl died on the way due to extreme heat. At the beginning of our journey, from Debdeb, we were told that the van will stop for no man until we get to our destination, but the driver stopped many times on the road to bribe soldiers and pay militias. It was at one of our stops that we informed the driver about the dead girl.

He asked all the women and girls to step down from the truck and move away from the corpse, then ordered the men to carry the body and place it under a small tree. For fear of not overcoming myself, I tried to be intrepid in every horror scene I saw. A woman, with tears in her eyes, offered her wrapper to cover the girl's body. The burial was so snappy, with just a surah and a hand of sand poured on her. Women and girls were not allowed to participate in the burial process; in fact, we were asked to back off for religious reasons.

As we continue our journey, I thought of all the people that may have been buried in such a manner—those people whose parents don't know their whereabouts. Those whose carcasses had been left as food for the vultures and other creatures. I wondered how many. You could tell from the driver's action that he's accustomed to dumping migrants that have died on the way. And no matter the status of the family you came from, we all travelled in destitute and like stateless folks searching for lands to enjoy fresh liberty. Fatoumatta held my left hand tightly as we passed through the wide desert and under lousy weather. I hated the smell of skin that very moment; the perspiration made it soggy.

After twenty-four hours of traveling, we went to a transit point in Libya with schools of pick-up trucks and hundreds of migrants in squalor from different parts of Africa. I even heard people communicating in some of our languages in Sierra Leone. According to the contractor from Debdeb, he told us the driver will transfer us to another van, which would take us to Tripoli, and he had honoured all the bills. As arranged, the driver transferred us to another truck and whispered a few words to our new driver. Not too long after, we left for Tripoli. But before we departed for Tripoli from that transiting point, Sainabou told us she didn't feel comfortable with the new driver.

"I don't trust him!" she repeated a few times, and Sainabou had never felt paranoid like that since we started the journey.

I became scared, and Fatoumatta too, I am sure; but we were left with no safe choice. "Let seek solace from Allah in prayers," Fatoumatta said. Of course, I read the twenty-third Psalm in my mind while the others read surah verbally.

Sainabou asked me to sit between her legs immediately after we climbed the other truck. Some minutes after we departed the transit point, I leaned on Sainabou and dozed off.

I woke up from my catnap with barrels to our heads and militias surrounding the truck. Several shots were fired up the air before the leader of the group in his broken English, ordered us to get down the track, and we did it in haste. He commanded us again to hand over all our money and all other valuables in our possession. Once almost all money and valuables had been collected from us, we were ordered to climb the van again after our eyes had been tied. Several gunshots were fired, and voices of men screamed for their lives, then the atmosphere became silent again.

"Lets move!" their leader shouted. The truck that was full of humans became very spacious. Only for us to get to an unknown location, we realized that five of us made it, including a five-year-old girl. The fifteen men, plus the driver may have been killed.

We walked through a damp room with two black women in chains, sitting hopelessly. The militia at our side shouted when we tried to slow down the queue to look at them. Through a very small corridor, we were asked to wait as we were called one by one to a very small room. I was seventh on the row, and all those who were before me never came out. *Have they killed them silently?* I asked myself. When it was my turn, Fatoumatta told me to be strong there. When I walked through the tiny corridor and entered the room, I realized that there was another door that led to a big hall. An A4 size paper with names of previous migrants was given to me to write down my name and age. After I wrote my information, a huge guy pointed to the other door to exit. Through that door, I was welcomed with chains to my hands and legs. I was walked to a corner by a man who looked like a giant. Both on my left and right side were people in chains: women and girls, but kids were left to roam around the hall.

Right beside me was Alberta—my dear Alberta, whose face I couldn't recognize at first sight. It was hard to believe what I saw. I called her name twice and calling her twice was to make sure it was her. I knew that very moment that her experience on the road had stolen her beauty.

"Where are the others?" in a whispering tone I asked her.

She gazed at me for some seconds before she laid her head on my shoulder and cried out, "They are all dead."

It wasn't shocking to me. In fact seeing Alberta was a miracle. The troubles on the road are a guarantee that many will die. Death is a kind friend for a lot of migrants. All of them are special to me, especially Sabel, whom I placed on a pedestal.

Earlier, I wished I joined their group because I thought the path they took was somehow safe, but the spirit of death follows all. Immediately, she asked me about the others. Fatoumatta entered with chains around her ankle. She managed to drag her legs until she got to us and tears broke out.

After the sobbing seized, Fatoumatta asked the same question. "Where are the others?"

Through the expression on Alberta's face, Fatoumatta already knew what her answer was going to be. "My darling Sabel, too?" Fatoumatta asked her again, and Alberta nodded her head.

As we were sobbing, Sainabou entered the hall—chained also. She wept as she dragged her feet towards us. With profuse tears from her eyes, Sainabou asked Alberta why Sabel and the others were not with her.

According to Alberta, Sabel died of complications, Grace was gang-raped and the two Sierra Leoneans that went with them were probably killed by the same militias—our captors. Alberta told us Grace ran out of money before they got to the transit point. After many disappointments from the calls she made home, they went to bed one night, and in the morning; Grace was found dead about three hundred meters away from them. The information that led to her death made no sense to us but was troubling.

The following day, the huge guy who chained me and probably all of us entered the hall with a tense face. Behind him were two other men and a woman in jillaroo, looking so strange. We shouted to stand up and look straight into their eyes while the woman walked around us striping us half-naked. The men walked around us squeezing our breasts and buttocks. A young teenager and I were asked to move forward. I knew they wanted to take me away from Fatoumatta and the others, and I would see them no more. I managed to drag myself and sat in front of Fatoumatta and squeezed myself between her legs, begging her not to let them take me away. Sainabou, Alberta, and Fatoumatta fought so hard to prevent them from taking me away, but one of the men hit them hard on their heads with a butt stock, and all three of them dropped down motionless. At that very moment, I thought they were dead. I never hoped to see them again. I was then believed to be on my own in that wasteland.

Right in the tiny room where we penned down our information before we entered the hall, the same paper was given to us to identify our info. The first time I raised my voice to speak to them and called them Satan's agents, I received a hot slap that made me content with my audibility. I verified my details and reluctantly moved with the brutal guy to another room, which was a little bit neater than the other.

I was in the same room with the two other ladies. I am certain they were both from Liberia and Mali, though they refused to disclose their nationalities to me. We were in the same boat, and we didn't know our fate. It was all migrants' wishes to be rid of the militias and their order.

A rifleman entered the room where we were kept with bowls of food and a jug of water. It was over thirty-eight hours without nourishment; I still had no appetite for food. In that state of trepidation, food heals nothing. Food could be one of the reasons I was going to face peril. My separation from the others means nothing but death.

The rifleman came back and met the food as he left them. I saw the disappointment on his face. Without saying a word, he left and returned with another militia who looked more fearful than him. Right to my head was a barrel of an AK47. "Eat!" he shouted at me. Since death was my only rescue and all I wanted, I become very obstinate.

"Eat! If you don't eat, I'll kill you!" the man screamed at me.

"Oh, death, how long have I been waiting for you! What kept you so long?" I smiled as I said these words. The long-waited rescuer was right on top of my head.

After some seconds, he slapped me instead of pulling the trigger. He waited again for another few seconds. When he realized I wasn't ready to eat at all, and I wasn't afraid of death, he slapped my head and walked off. Glancing through the window, I saw the militias moving two corpses from the hall. My thought went to Fatoumatta, Alberta, and Sainabou—did they survive the heavy hit of the butt stock?

I was isolated from the other two ladies just after the terrible man left, until sunset, and then a man came with manacles and a bottle of water. "You, water?" he asked me. As the darkness overtook the light, both my hands were pinioned, my mouth taped up, and my eyes tied. I had no idea where we were and where we were handed to. Two people took me out of the building and drove me straight to the East for over two hours, then routed me to the north for another few hours.

When shall I see my home again? Would I ever go to see her again? When I die, would life permit my soul to visit Mama Salone? It was my wish to run away from my aunt's demand but never dreamt of perishing in a deserted place.

I felt drowsy throughout that four-hour journey. I avoided falling asleep; I will try to force my hands out of the manacle to feel the hurt. My watch alarmed me at midnight, my time to pray. While praying, the van pulled over, and the person sitting in front of the car went out. I heard them discussing for more than five minutes, and then I was transferred to another van.

I almost died of suffocation. It was as if I'd placed my nose in a chimney pot. The two people sitting at my sides, the one on the passenger's seat, and the driver—predominantly men—were smokers. We pulled over again, the place I thought was our final destination. All of them went out of the car to join the cheering crown, except the one who sat on my left hand. After the three others were gone, the guy on my left side elbowed me and told me not to sleep. I wasn't sleeping. In fact, I never slumbered. In a well-spoken English language, he told me to nod my head if yes or shake my head if no.

The first thing he told me was, "Don't worry, you're not going to die." These were some of the questions and comments that he made, as far as I could remember.

"How old are you." he asked me

"Where are you from?" he asked again

"Are you a virgin?" he raised his voice to scare me.

Our bosses love virgins...

"Do you know how to have sex?"

You black Africans know how to give good sex.

I never moved my head to any of his questions asked or statements made. If I tried to remember some of the distasteful interrogations and comments that he made, my day would spoil. Though I paid great attention to all that he said, how trivial they were, it gave me a clue of the challenges ahead. I could feel my body trimmed down drastically.

I heard a voice of a lady walking toward me. She untapped my mouth and said, "Hello, my friend. My name is Aafa. I know you need water. Here! Drink and preserve your life."

"Do you have liquid that will harm my life?" I asked her.

She giggled and said, "We the inhabitants of this land don't take lives, we give life."

"Do you have a daughter?" I asked her.

"Yes, I do!" she answered.

"Would you like to see her manacled like this?" I asked her again.

I never heard her voice again. I expectedly waited for her response, but she never did.

The men returned later with a cigarette and alcohol smell. Just five minutes after we left that point, the automobile became noisy with snoring from two to three men.

I don't tell a falsehood. If I do, I may have intentionally told you the hard truth. One preacher once told me that nobody has gone to hell and returned. Well, I have been there. I have lived on the darkest side of hell. I never thought I would have the opportunity to share this with anyone. My kids never believe that the paths they thoughts would lead to success would end up being a path to perdition, punishment, and death.

As the journey continued to an unknown destination, I recited the twenty-third Psalm over and over again. We passed through several checkpoints with baritone voices, and not one of those checkpoints checked our vehicle. I resisted sleep for many hours, finally, I slept off.

Chapter 9

As we continued our hazardous drive to nowhere, I realized that death may not come, and the perils possibly will arrive. As my hands were still chained, my legs manacled and eyes were still tied, my mouth was sealed, the only active sense was my ears. My instinct could tell me the kind of environment we were in. My sense of hearing communicated to me when we got to a big town, probably a city. Since then, I knew there was hope, though it will be tedious and tiring.

We drove for almost an hour before we finally went to a very quiet part in the urban area, then I was transferred to a car. Just five minutes' drive from where I was transferred, we entered a gated compound. I felt like a sheep being taken to the slaughterhouse. When we entered the compound, my hands were unchained, and the manacle around my legs was removed. Right in front of their boss, my face was unbound. With a smile on his face, he squeezed my breast and buttocks, just like they did to us at the warehouse.

The fat man—their boss, I thought—nodded his head and a woman came from the back and held on to my hand and led me to a room undercellar. The woman's name is Chibinobim, possibly from Benin, Ghana, or Nigeria, because she spoke exactly like Grace. I never thought I would receive encouraging words from the devil's agent, but I heard it.

"If you comply with them, you are going to be safe," she said.

"Comply with what?" I immediately asked her.

"You would know it's just a simple task," she replied.

"Know when? What simple task?" I asked.

She went silent until the security behind us returned to the sitting room. I was wondering why they would chain a girl just to do a modest job. In the corridor to the rooms, she turned around and told me that if I am good in bed and willingly ready to have sex with customers, it was possible to have my freedom when they regain trice the money they bought me. I marvel at the hateful desire she took to tell me about sex with multiple men and freedom after physically and mentally ruining what made me a girl. As we continued walking through the corridor, I saw other girls with miserable faces standing at the door to their rooms.

We got to a room at the end of the corridor; in there were two other girls and a woman in her late thirties. Of course, Chibinobim was older than her. The beds were of boarding school types and the wardrobes too. I was welcomed by the girls with painful tears. I was taken directly to the shower, where Chibinobim asked me to take off my clothes, including my pants, and promised to get me some new ones. When I went out of the shower, one of the girls in the room gave me pink pants, a hot-pant, and a transparent half top, which I strongly rejected. She told me I had no option; it was either I put them on or remain nude the rest of my stay there.

An hour later, I had the privilege to sit with the elderly woman amongst us. And I had the freedom to ask him some of my unanswered questions. She told me we were sex slaves, and that I should be ready to sexually satisfy a male whenever I am called, and girls around my age were highly likely going to stay there forever. She also told me about some who were killed because they resisted their predators and those who may have suffered from schizophrenia and committed suicide.

While she was explaining to me that faithful afternoon, Chibinobim knocked at the door and asked me to follow her. She took me to a very tiny room with a pile of boxes. "Open any box and get some new wears for yourself!" she said to me.

The boxes were filled with uncomfortable dresses that show out my thighs, nipples, and even my breasts. The same I saw on the girls in the room. I had to ask her for modest dresses, but she told me their visitors may be religious, but they are not holy; their primary reason for going there is sex.

"What if, I refuse to put them on?" I asked her

"Then you go nude the rest of your life here," she responded.

"For the rest of my life?"

"Throughout my stay here, I haven't seen a sweet-looking girl as you walk out of this compound alive, but their corpses do."

When I asked her about the duration she had been there, she told me that the Mediterranean Sea gave us the green light. In there, we were shackled with no metals, bound from living on our planet. As far as I could remember, the longest-serving sex slave in the building was a Togolese lady called Blessing.

On my first night there, we were invited to a very big hall upstairs, and we were to go there topless or with short tops. Because of the conditions, I refused to join the other females. Their leader, who became stung by my behaviour, ordered one of his boys to drag me out of my room. The man brutally did. We were gathered at the big hall every morning and evening to see if they had any missed persons.

After the inspection, the two young girls, possibly from Ghana, were asked to wait, but we were asked to return to our room. The girls didn't return until after two hours. They returned crying, but never explained what had happened to them.

The following night, after the evening inspection, I was asked to stay, as they did to the others the previous night. I was taken to a very fortified room with Chibinobim. That day I heard the head of our captives called her Aretta. Chibinobim, or Aretta, encouraged me to cooperate with anyone that entered the room after she had left. And she promised the person was going to be very nice to me. Immediately after she had left, with the door shut behind her, a huge fat man entered the room, and the door was shut behind him. That was the very moment I understood what was happening. I tried to rush out of the room, but the door was locked. After I resisted him for over ten minutes, he tried to overpower me. Though he was healthy, I was skilful. I could tell from his face he was furious and disappointed because he couldn't get between my legs. I was right behind him as he left the room. I knew I was in double; trouble denying the visitor access to my sexual parts and my desire at that moment was to get out of harm's way. I had to boldly walk to the women's room and wait for nothing but my death so I could have my freedom at last.

A few moments later, two juvenile offenders bashed into our room and dragged me out in front of the other juveniles who were half-naked by then. All those moments are engraved in my memory. I was beaten mercilessly until I lost consciousness. I later learned that that was what they do to any female who resisted having sex with a visitor is to instil fear in us. Nobody knew how jaded life was for me, only me. I would never be able to recover from the pains I acquired from that voyage.

The day the leader of the group died, which I heard from Chibinobim, my eyes were covered and two of the men took me to a sacred well-fortified chamber in the house. When they left, the door was completely jammed. About ten minutes later, Chibinobim entered the room. That was the first time I had the opportunity to talk to her face to face after I was brutally beaten. This is how the conversation between us went:

"The last time I had the opportunity to talk with you directly like this, I advised you to cooperate. I was so kind to you. Wasn't I?" she asked me.

"The last time I was so unfortunate to talk with you directly like this, you left me to die. Am I here again to face my death the second time?" I responded.

"I have daughters, who are of the same age as you, and one of them is in the hands of this people I am reluctantly working for and the other is at large. Her life depends on my cooperation here, do you understand that?" she asked.

I never thought she was working under duress. She seemed excited and willing to do the job. She was so vigilant as if she were willing to seek the job.

She went on to say if she had the power, none of us {the migrants} would breathe under that roof. With tears from her eyes, she moved a bit closer to me and said, "I know you haven't been touched and that you are preserving yourself for an unknown future. The state of your virginal situation doesn't determine your future. Corpses of juveniles like you had been dragged out of that gate—beautiful souls that the world would hate to miss. Just let them do what they want to your body and hope that someday you shall see the sunlight again."

I looked right into her eyes and said, "If a death has finally come, I welcome it. What's worth living? All my friends are dead!"

"Then decline death and live to tell the story to somebody someday," she said.

I had no time to give it a thought, even when she left me to my fate. I made moves to follow her outside the room, but I was pushed back inside by two militias. When the man who was to take me to bed arrived, I became more adamant. The visitor didn't spend time handling me; he got mad and left the room. When the information got to their boss, he ordered his boys to beat me up mercilessly, raped, and kill me.

Maybe because they saw that I had no hope of recovery, I was taken out of the compound, possibly miles away, and dumped in a nearby town.

Chapter 10

Address!

Hell

Hello Dear,

You are among the dozens of corpses that had been taken away to be thrown in the desert. Even though I have it written in my mind that corpses don't read, I still dare to write and place this note around the area that made us called female so it could hardly be seen by the dumpers. I believe one, among the dozens of corpses, may resurrect. Miracles could happen in bad places.

If you are never restored to life, and there is no life after death, it means life is unfair. And if you never resuscitate, but there is life after death, I pray our souls to meet and dine ever after. But if you die and are resurrected, tell the people of the future world what you've seen and heard here. We are in obscurity and have no hope of seeing the light.

As I have always done, I give dead people a description of my daughter, Mercy. She first disappeared before me, and I was abducted while searching for her. If they could find her after death, let her know that her mother is between life and death. Please, if you see a huge 4ft 2in girl in her early teen with round eyes, a small mouth, and a snub nose with an alto voice, tell her that her mother is a walking dead. Even though it is highly unlikely for any abducted female to survive the torture here, there is likely death after life, and there is life after death. However, if you find my daughter among the living, please encourage her to go back home to stay with her uncle at Oyo.

I have been forcefully employed to lure and encourage women and girls to do something beyond their wishes, turning a house into a home for lechers, cleaning up females after they had been sexually brutalized by men, giving hope to people in a hopeless situation, and above all forced to feel contented.

May your soul find peace.

These were exactly the words I read from a letter I found inside my pants, possibly placed there by Chibinobim.

I regained consciousness in a very strange house and a strange old Arab woman watching over me. Fagged out, but yet tried to move.

"Min fadlik astalaq," the old woman said as she ran out of the room and returned with a cup of water and a teenager around my age.

"Where am I?" I asked.

To my surprise, the boy replied to me in English, encouraging me to drink first.

"Drink!" he said. "You are safe here."

Though they were kind to me, I couldn't trust anyone at that very moment. The boy told me they were my family I had never met. And as he was talking, the old woman who happens to be her grandmother was cuddling me with a smile on her face.

"Drink first. Your life is better than the information you are seeking for!" the boy said again.

For some days, I couldn't feel relieved because I wasn't sure where I was, who those people were, or whether they were working for some people or they are just Good Samaritans. *Could it be they are working indirectly for my abductors?* I asked myself.

One day, after I drank a bitter medicine from a phial, I was alone with the old woman's grandson; then I asked him how his grandma knew I was in the desert. He gazed at me for a second and smiled. He told me his grandma is a phenom in traditional medication and she is a mysterious woman in other ways. Sometimes she does things that he could not figure out how. According to him, it was his grandma who suggested they should walk around the town one morning, and she wanted to view the surroundings, which was very unusual. They found me half-dead at the side of the road close to a bakery. I can't remember all of the things we discussed at that moment, but I felt relieved knowing that I have been physically freed. I wasn't sure if my abductors knew I was still alive or if they wanted the sun and sand to polish me off.

My room, so poky, was still a comfort zone for me. On my seventeenth night with my new family and my new home, I thought about whether I should return home or whether I should continue my hopeless journey. The reasons I gathered to move ahead were much more important than the reasons to return. I didn't even know how I got to where I was. Abdul Quddus—which is the name of the old woman's grandson—and the old lady were with me almost the rest of the day on the eighteenth day, seeking to know where a teenager like me could leave her country alone on such an age.

Questions about my plans after recovery came up. They wanted to know whether I would continue staying with them and start a new life, return home and continue my old life, or continue my hazardous journey. I was fifteen years then.

After I missed my period, which I thought was a scary thing, I thought about what I have learned in school that a female's menstrual period can delay. It became alarming when I had a painful breast, sensitive to smell and tiredness scooped in. I knew something was wrong with me on my nineteenth day in that town. The following day, after Jadati had spent quality time with me, she went out and asked her grandson to let me know I was pregnant. "Was I going to make it to my destination or perished in Libya?" I immediately asked myself.

There was no change of mood on both the woman and her lad when I told them my desire to endure my voyage.

Once I fully recovered, as I was preparing to embark on my journey to Tripoli, the old woman told me many things that I needed to be aware of when I get to Tripoli. She also gave me the contact of her son-in-law in Tripoli, who was working for the United Nations recognized government. From where I was to go to Tripoli is the same distance from there to the Libya border with Tunisia. I cried in my last hour with that generous family, and besides their big-heartedness, the last food they served me looked precisely the same as the one they served me the very moment they separated me from the others. It reminded me of my life as a commodity. The woman said through the interpretation of her son that I am always welcome in her home.

Covered in a veil by my new guardian, she walked me to a nearby bus station and warned me, through her grandson, that I shouldn't be distracted by anything. Though my main objective was to cross the giant sea, I had no idea how and where. Some of the pieces of advice given to me by Jadati were to avoid jam-packed areas and avoid talking to people and isolated places. I couldn't say a single word to anyone until I got to the bus stop in Tripoli.

At the bus station, I saw a couple of women in colours. They ignored me a couple of times when I tried to converse with them.

Before the sun disappeared, I decided to telephone Jadati's in-law, who picked me up at the bus station.

Bachar, who anglicised his name to Bachman, lived in a very big, modernized house, in downtown Tripoli. He was one of those who took arms against the former leader. I heard it from the horse's mouth when he requested I dine with him on his dining table. I never expected to meet him alone at the house, and I hate putting up in such environs. After I had explained all that I went through from Sierra Leone to Libya, he seemed to pity me and promised to help me cross over. It was one of the best news I heard after I made it half-dead from that doom. At midnight, I heard someone moving up and down in the sitting room, so I couldn't sleep until the whole house was silent. The following night, after showing how generous he was, he entered my room at night without having me and asked me to make love with him if I wanted to make it to Europe. He tried to convince me with different offers, but I still denied him, so he said sorry for incommoding me. As a gentle way of telling strangers to leave your house, he told me he was traveling to another town for official reasons, and that he wasn't comfortable letting me stay in his house alone. He seethed gently back to his room.

As one could sense the disappointment in his face, he drove me back to the bus station where he picked me up first thing the following morning. I spent the night at the bus station behind a relaxation point. Though the decision of Bachman was irksome, it was the best decision available.

In the morning, I had the opportunity to see the same ladies that I saw the previous day. One specific one with interlaced hair looked familiar to me, so I walked up to her. She was very joyful to see and chat with me. Spending about five nights with them, I was amazed at their joviality. The things that were hidden from me almost got me entangled in their mess. The night their landlord returned from his five-day trip, he ordered one of my friends to go with him.

He didn't return until 3:00 a.m. in the morning.

Another night, their landlord requested that I go with him to his room as he commanded the sub-Saharan lady. We argued for some minutes, and I responded to him, not in a ladylike manner. After he left and promised to return, I decided to ask Bernadette, the other lady, what was going on. I became concerned about some of the statements he uttered. "They didn't tell you? Your friends didn't tell you on which terms and conditions they are here?"

Bernadette told me that the man asked them not to pay for accommodation, but they should allowed him to take them to bed as he wishes, and since they were homeless, and they had no money to afford an apartment they had to agree to the condition.

I dared to sit them down and told them all I have seen, have heard, and the folk I have lost since the beginning of my journey.

The whole room went silent. They may have never thought someone could go through what I went through and survived. And a 15-year-old pregnant girl.

They too shared their stories with me. Bernadette was a gangling youth in her late twenties. She was either from the Anglophone area in Cameroon, or she was a Ghanaian, or both. She told me her husband had to drain his business for her to face the giant sea, and that she won't return home in shame.

Fatmata Kouassi's has a similar story to mine, but she was running away from her early marriage. She was an Ivorian, a beautiful type. The boldness they had to share their reasons with me prompted me to share mine with them. When they knew that I ran away from being mutilated by the female secret society, I was mocked and denounced. Throughout my time with Fatoumatta's group, I never disclosed my reasons for leaving my home to join them.

In the end, they shared their plans to cross the sea, and I shared my wishes. Yes, my wishes. I had no plans because I knew no way. Bernadette told me about a smuggler in town who was rarely seen around for security reasons, but she knew where to find him. And the fact that I couldn't agree to the condition of their landlord, I left the apartment and made a home on the streets. Right behind the relaxation point, I found it far from the madding crowd, and since it was the hustling ground for Bernadette and her friend Isha, I had the opportunity to see and chat with them daily.

As advised by my Jadati, I was always on the veil which was one of the reasons the chef marvelled at me and introduced me to her boss. I had the opportunity to work as a cleaner about three hundred meters from the place I called home. I laboured there for only a month, and I quit. I don't know if it was because of me, but the owner of the restaurant introduced a labyrinth of rules that discomforted me. While labouring there, I was opportune to meet with a very nice Orthodox Egyptian; through her, I met another lady that took me to a genuine smuggler. I introduced Bernadette and Isha to the smuggler too.

Within the same week, the smuggler took us to a warehouse near the sea. I was blessed to meet a person I thought was a ghost: Fatoumatta.

"Fatoumatta?" I shouted.

We hugged each other and we shed tears together. As we gazed at each other, she knew the question I wanted to ask. "They couldn't make it out there alive," she said to me. "They all survived the gun butt, but Sainabou and Grace couldn't survive from the barrel when they tried to escape." According to her, she warned them not to make the move.

Fatoumatta was bought by another sex-trafficker eleven days after I was taken away from them, and five days after Grace and Sainabou were shot dead while trying to escape. On the way to her unknown destination, they had an accident. Nonetheless, she was safe with little bruises, but her traffickers were badly hurt. She trekked deep into the desert hoping to find safety, and she was recaptured again by another group that only demanded money from her family back home.

With Fatoumatta at my side, I became renewed in the same old situation. I shared with Fatoumatta the money I received from generous Jadati. From other stranded migrants like us, she bought me black sneakers and clothes in mint condition. I saw a sign of hope from the smile Fatoumatta gave me at any time she gazed at me. During a relaxing time, she would tell me about the beautiful culture of the Gambia people and how much it had played a vital role in her life. It was at that moment she thought of the reason I disappeared from the eyes of my aunt.

"Are you still proud of your decision?"

It was at the wrong time, and at the wrong place to be asked such a question. "I will forever be proud of my decision." With smugness on my face, I answered her.

The first and last disagreement between Fatoumatta and me was to lie about the reason why I ran away from home. I told her it's degrading to lie and embarrassing not to tell the truth.

"You're not proud of me, are you?" I asked her. It was a question she never answered, and she dodged it twice.

"Why do you hate the process that transforms us from girlhood to womanhood? Do you want to remain a girl forever? If real women here heard this, you would be mocked," she said to me. She told me the white folks would kick my butt back to Africa if they heard I ran away from being initiated into the Bondo Secret Society. "Which white fool would hail me for being a coward?" she continued. I became completely silent, which prompted her to ask me why I chose not to undergo the initiation.

I told her about the zillions of brains that have died through the initiation process. About the cutting of our private parts with knives that are contaminated with tetanus, about the women and girls that are dying of healthy snags which they got through the wounding, about women and children's rights that have been violated. "Who could praise a filthy custom like the Female Genital Mutilation? As some believe that some of us are running away from destitution, and then to me, FGM is my penury," I commented. I didn't even mention the hostile blood loss, the complications during childbearing, and other infections. She left my presence for a while without having me.

To you reading my story, I'd rather face death than be mutilated. Female Genital Mutilation is an injurious and destructive practice, through which females and their babies are dying. The females before us, who stood up against such practice, were silenced, neglected, or banished. It is as if Africa is meant for only mutilated women and girls. If the white men were to kick me out of their land, as Fatoumatta told me, I shall still be proud of myself. Nobody would be prouder of me but me.

Fatoumatta's foremothers were also mutilators, including her late grandmother.

I had wanted to continue the discussion with her, but we were interrupted by news that about one hundred migrants may have died in the sea the previous night. It was never a piece of bad news to any of us, I think because we tried to adapt ourselves to evil news from the sea. Our agent, who came after the bad news deliverer left, never said anything about the capsized but to remind us to prepare to cross.

We were on board the boat three days later when a very intelligent girl died. She was buried in a smartish pace. Yes, the hundred or so people that died; yes, the death of the brainy lassie; and yes, the sick, was something to worry about. Yet it never stole the desperations, hopes, and confidence we had to reach the land of freedom and wealth, as we've been told.

The night before we got on the boat, fear overcame Fatoumatta. She spoke about death multiple times that evening. I sensed defeat in her words. After she shared her immediate family's contact with me, she asked me to do the same. I had no family contact by then, and besides, I had wanted my location to be kept in secret, even if I fell into the sea. The reason she gave me was that we would contact each other's family if anything bad happened. Since I joined their group, it was at that very moment that Fatoumatta asked me if my parents were aware of my crossing. I could still remember the wobbling of my voice as I responded emotionally to her.

It is known that migrants like us are running from destitute countries, but that abandoned warehouse, which we called a waiting room, was full of females and males running from their homes that hate their identities. Some of their identities, in some very primitive societies, are considered cursed, so they are muzzled by their government' laws. So, I became one of those who were searching for a home that would value what I brought to the world, not the decision I made for my good.

We were moved to another warehouse very close to the sea. It was to our surprise that we met Emmanuel. He greeted me first and later Fatoumatta, who acted stone-deaf. She was so furious at him that very moment, and her anger was extended to me for responding to his greetings. The regret on his face was vivid. Fatoumatta never said a word to him until death separated them.

There, the most energetic men, including Emmanuel, were given a small lecture on how to operate the machine. I had to listen attentively to every detail given to them by our smugglers, and I prayed fervently in my heart to sit next to the operators.

Unfortunately for me...well, it wasn't my decision because I was a female; in fact, a girl and Fatoumatta denounced the idea to be around that part of the boat.

Getting on the boat at 3 a.m. was a time I never expected. I was more confident and braver when the hour came, but I became nervous and worried when I found out that the boat was plastic made. I thought we were to use a boat made of wood or iron like I had seen in Sierra Leone. I was very dissatisfied and became more troubled than Fatoumatta. I lost the comfort I once had to sit in the cockpit of the boat. Fatoumatta walked straight to the deepest area of the boat—a position where we couldn't see the water. People prayed in languages and to gods I have never heard of. I held on to Fatoumatta's trousers, and she held on to mine until death separated us.

Ever since we boarded the boat and set sail, I wasn't in charge of my emotions and many others too. I thought it wasn't a tedious voyage, thus I pleaded passionately in my mind for us to disembark soon enough.

After sailing for about a couple of hours, we couldn't see where we were coming from, and our destination, the plastic boat, started deflating, and the torchlight of the operator began malfunctioning. We were told we shouldn't worry when we get into a situation like that; highly likely humanitarian boats would come to our rescue before the worse may happen. As the deflation continued, migrants started losing their holds, spaces became limited—all hell broke loose. That very moment was the last hour for many beautiful souls. We started screaming and calling for help from people we couldn't see. Fatoumatta asked me to hold firmly to a rope tied to the boat. It was so dramatic and noisy that I can't remember the many things that happened. We had 150 migrants, at the very most and only around 50 remained as fright continued.

I inflexibly seized on Fatoumatta, as she cautioned me many times not to let go of her. The boat became a swimming pool, and the woman with her baby next to me was swept away, but I held firmly to the cord, screaming Fatoumatta's name. I struggled to turn to the other side of the boat; all I saw was Fatoumatta struggling to stay alive out of the boat. She dived first, second, and the third time. I never saw her again. Emmanuel was nowhere to be seen.

This is all I can remember that happened inside the boat.

When I regained consciousness on board a humanitarian ship, I was told I made it with two others. I was eager to meet the other two migrants that made it with me.

"Do you know their names?" I asked the nurse.

"Only one!" she answered.

"What is her name?" I anxiously asked her.

"His name is James," she responded.

"Did you see Fatoumatta?" I asked her.

She left the position where she was standing, went to my bedside, and gently pushed my chest to the bed. "Rest, and when you recover you shall ask all the questions that you have," she said.

I forced myself up again and told her how important Fatoumatta was to me. "Unfortunately, they are both late thirties males. You should be joyful that you and your unborn child are safe," she said. I thought of Emmanuel, but he was just in his early twenties.

I burst into tears. I cried my heart out in pain.

Through all the myriad difficulties on the road, Fatoumatta and the others never made it.

Some hours later, I managed to walk out of my room and stood by the rails, glazing on the off chance to see Fatoumatta's corpse. As I stood there, I thought about all the geniuses that have been trapped by the monster sea. In the dock I saw some other migrants rescued from other boats; they were all smiling and embracing one another while the corpse of other migrants was dancing around the ship. Right there the spirit of sadness that held me since I heard of Fatoumatta's death was silenced. I smiled, knowing that other people were rescued that day.

One of our rescuers called me and gave me the small bottle where I placed Jadati's address, Chibi's letter, and Fatoumatta family's contact. I thought I should put it in a small bottle and tie it around my waist before we embarked the boat.

As we got closer to the shore of Italy, I asked myself, *Is this land worth the thousands of beautiful souls that have died to see her?*

Printed in Great Britain
by Amazon

13234722R00102